TO AIDE A WOLF

USA TODAY BESTSELLING AUTHOR
JESSICA CAGE

Contents

One

He smelled like ass and had a face to match. At least that was until his body shifted from the fur covered beast into something more appealing to the eye. Muscled, coated in deep brown skin, and tatted with scars.

The moonlight washed across her dark skin, as Kiora sat carefully perched on the treetop, and watched as the injured wolf's body transformed. It was a risky decision for him to shift, especially considered how exposed he was, but she understood why he did it. His body would heal faster in human form and if he weren't hurt too badly, he could move beneath the cover of the nearby bushes. It would not be enough to hide his scent, but it might save his life.

Her pointed ears twitched as she listened to the area checking to see if there were any other people, wolves or otherwise. Besides a few small animals and birds, she heard nothing. Still, she remained cautious, and watched him from afar.

She should have taken him out while he was vulnerable. The wolf didn't belong in their territory, but curiosity had her in its grips. Like most, Kiora had never witnessed a wolf shift, but it was something she always wondered about. Of all the supernatural species in their world, wolves were the ones she knew most about outside of her own. It was part of her job to know everything about the enemy. And for the fairies, wolves were at the top of the list of threats.

Kiora was a fairy guard. Her duty was to protect her people from threats. For decades, battles ensued between the two species. After some wolves decided the answer to their troubles with the vampires was to attack the fairies. Ingesting fairy blood allowed them to absorb the magic of the beings and gave them the strength and ability to better handle the vampires. Funny how they didn't see the irony of what they were doing. They wanted to stop the vampires from ravishing their land, so they did the same thing to the fairies.

After twenty-seven years of bloodshed, the fairies finally discovered a way to fight back and did so by threatening the wolf's need for a connection to the moon. Though the wolves had developed to no longer depend on the moon for their physical transformation, their magic still had a connection to its power. The fairies threw up a blanket of magic that severed that connection and refused to remove it until the wolves agreed on a treaty.

This didn't take long considering how the disconnect made it harder for the wolves to control their shifts and left them vulnerable to the vampire attacks. With this threat in place, the wolves made a treaty with the fairies that they would never harm another fairy or step foot on their land again.

Sixty-two years later, Kiora looked down on the first wolf to come near their home. He lay there bloodied, beaten, covered in evidence of a brutal battle, and far too close to her home for comfort. She leaned in so she could get a better look as his body completed the shift. Her fascination had her hanging from the tree, eyes wide like a child at the desert table.

Kiora had an analytical mind that made constant mental notes of everything she witnessed. She committed to memory the sounds the bones made, cracks, breaks and splintering snaps rang out before the cool whisper of repair as the jagged pieces reformed within his body. Her eyes caught every detail of the way his paws became feet and hands. The fur pulled back to reveal dark brown skin. His claws retracted and powerful hands gripped the grass covered ground while his face previously elongated to house the powerful jaw, shortened. The twisted expression the motion left on his face made her stomach turn. She smacked her hand over her mouth to muffle the sound of her own gag.

When it was done. The stench of the wolf softened and the musk of the man, woody and deep, carried to her by the gentle wind. She peered down at the man and frowned, not because she was worried but because, despite the blood, bruises, and scars that covered him, he wasn't nearly as ugly as she imagined him to be. He had a short afro of light brown hair, a square jaw, and a powerful frame with muscles that flexed against his pain.

She ignored thoughts of his solid ass and contemplated what she should do next. The bylaws stated she was to report back immediately and alert the others that there was a threat on the territory, and she almost did that, but then she heard a soft moan cross his lips followed by an urgent prayer to the goddess.

"Goddess, if you hear me, I beg of you protect my brother in the way I could not." He coughed and blood spilled from his lip. "Save his soul and return him home to our family where he belongs."

The moment before he spoke, she'd been prepared to do her job. Capture the wolf and report the troubling find to her superiors. But hearing his prayer for help, inspired a new hesitation and her mind left her physical self to return to the memory of a time she hoped one day wouldn't cut so deeply.

The last time she saw her sister, Safir smiled. Her laughter rang out as she headed out with the convoy. She was always so happy and lighthearted. It's likely why she never made it back home. Safir looked for the best in people. She trusted too easily, despite her sister's warnings.

During her convoy, Safir was to blend in with the human population of Beinte, a city with over three million souls and a feeding ground for vampires. She was there to gather information about a new disease and find out if there was any threat to the fairy community. Her findings were that the sickness would not affect the fairies. She called in her report and told the superiors that her team would return the next night.

The next day, one person returned. One. Bloodied and choking on a nightmarish fear.

May. He told them of a massacre. The team celebrated their successful trip by going out to an event where hundreds of humans gathered. They realized too late that the place was crawling with vampires. At first, they were snatching humans, but when they realized there were fairies in the mix, the simple feeding turned gruesome. May was the only one to make it out alive.

Kiora pleaded with the superiors to allow her to go to Beinte and find her sister.

"Please, Safir is still out there. I know it." Kiora cried. "She's a survivor. She is out there waiting for me."

Despite her efforts to prove herself capable, they denied her request.

Her mind released her from the memory of her grief and the echoes of her sister's laughter, and Kiora looked down on the bloodied man and watched as he attempted to crawl beneath the cover of the bushes. She felt sorry for him.

The echoes of her own grief inspired something deeper within her. She empathized with him and couldn't help but imagine this man was just as close to his brother as she was to her sister. And then, against her better judgement, she decided she would give him the chance that she pleaded for, but never got. If there was a way that he could save his brother, she would allow it.

Kiora landed with a soft thud three feet from the man after leaping from the tree. Though her footfall was light, his tensed with the recognition that someone was nearby. Realizing how dangerous it was to be sneaking up on a werewolf, Kiora proceeded with caution.

"I'm here to help you." Kiora held her hands up, not that he could see her with his back to her. She kept her voice calm as she spoke. "I know you have no reason to trust me, but the same goes for me. You're hurt badly and if you stay here, someone will find you. Now, if that's whoever you were fighting before or if it's my people, it will not end well for you. I shouldn't be doing this, but I want to help you if you will let me."

The man remained silent, though she knew he was aware of her. His breathing had changed to an even pace, and she imagined he was likely considering his next move. His injuries were too great for him to shift again, which meant he couldn't get away. He turned his head and looked at her. One eye swollen so badly he could not open it to see her.

"Okay," he said through a bloody cough before he passed out.

"Great." Kiora looked down at the unconscious man, thanked the goddess for her connection to the earth, and grabbed him by the ankles.

It took twenty minutes, but she carefully dragged his limp body across the ground to a place that was once as familiar to her as her own home. They called it the cove. Kiora found the cove with her sister when they were young girls. It was an old fox hole they dug out, expanded ten times over, and reinforced

6

it with their magic over the years. It was their home away from home and where she hid for the first six months after her sister disappeared.

There was so much of their magic blended in with the place that few others knew it was there. Any other person, fairy or otherwise, could stand right at the mouth of it and never notice it was there. That was the best place she could think of to house the wounded wolf.

They decorated the inside with flowers, fabrics, jewels, and anything else sparkly they could find. They covered the walls with fabrics borrowed from their mother and in the back, there were several chests filled with unique collections they called their treasures. One was a literal box of rocks while another held their favorite blankets for the nights, they could convince their mother to allow them to stay and watch the stars.

After she got him inside and pushed him on top of the small cot made of a collection of leaves, hay, and moss, she stood back and laughed. There was more than enough space for both her and her sister, and yet his long body looked cramped. She returned to where she found him and quickly brushed away the path his body created when she dragged him across the ground.

Kiora told herself this was a time to be analytical. She looked over his body, not because she found the muscle attractive, but because it was a moment to research the physical attributes of a potential enemy. She looked at his short afro, matted with his own blood because it shocked her that his fur didn't match the texture of his hair. Every detail she noted about the man who looked to be over six feet tall and lay in front of her, completely nude, was strictly research.

Her curiosity peaked even further when his wounds slowly healed. The bruising around his ribs lost their deep purple color, and the swelling in his face receded. She tried to calculate in her mind how long it would take for him to fully recover. She didn't imagine it would be more than a couple of days.

"I can keep you safe here for that long." she muttered, then jumped as the four marks tattooed on her inner wrist lit up.

Kiora jumped up and ran outside of the hideaway before tapping her inner wrist.

"Kiora here." She looked up at the dark sky and wished the stars offered her a simple solution to her newfound problem.

"You're late. Is everything okay?" The airy voice called out to her. "I was worrying about you."

"Um, yeah." she glanced at the entrance to the space where the werewolf slept. "Just got wrapped up in things here. I'm headed back now."

"Good, because the boss is agitated. Something to do with the wolves."

"On my way." Kiora pressed her finger on the second mark and the connection ended. "Fuck."

She hesitated for a moment, questioning if she'd made the right choice when she helped the wolf. Either way, there was no time to take it back. She only hoped that no one would find out her secret. Kiora spread her wings, black with blue and silver webbing, and took flight, lifting above the trees to head home.

Two

Nervous feet touched the ground at the edge of the outer city. Rege was the home of the fairies. Surrounded by a thick circle of trees and magically protected to make sure that no threats, like the werewolf hidden at the border's edge, made it inside. The city had a maze of structures, some made, and others grown. Without a guide, an outsider would lose their way within minutes of entering, but Rege spoke to the people who lived there. It moved with the fairies and guided them through its passages without issue.

Kiora tucked her wings back and straightened the collar of the skintight material that aided her movements while on duty. The material matched her wings. Black with blue and silver webbing that covered it from neck to toe. They made every fairy guard's gear to match their wings. It helped with blending in with their surroundings.

"Kiora." The same airy voice that spoke over her communicator called from the open door to the guard post. A tower at the edge of their home where their superiors, the heads of the guards, lived indefinitely. Roe, her friend and fellow guard, stood at the entrance dressed in her fit that matched the deep reds and oranges of her wings. "We're waiting. You think you might want to come inside?"

"Oh, yeah. Sorry." Kiora jogged over to the open door.

"What's going on with you today, girl?" Roe asked, flipping her long red braids over her shoulder. "It's not like you to be late. You're usually the first one here."

"I know." Kiora adjusted her braided bun as she stepped across the threshold. "I've had a lot on my mind today."

"Did whatever you have on your mind cause you to roll through horse shit?" Roe pinched her wide nose and spoke in a nasal sound. "Not to be mean, but you stink."

"I, uh," Kiora sniffed her collar, annoyed she hadn't considered the wolf's smell might stick to her. "If you must know, I had an uneven landing jumping from a tree." She lied.

"Well, let's hope this meeting is short and you can go shower up." Roe smacked Kiora on the shoulder and sniffed her hand as if the smell would transfer to her.

The two headed inside the tower and quickly found their way to the meeting hall where ninety percent of the available guards were.

"This must be serious," Kiora whispered to Roe. "I've never seen this many guards gathered at once."

The meeting room where the guards met was a large crescent shape big enough to fit five hundred people. They lined the seats evenly in the curved space with each row on another level descending to the front of the room where, at the center, was the superior bench where the leaders of the guards sat and addressed the others. Portraits of the fairy royals and depictions of their home lined the walls as a reminder of what they protected. On the outer wall, was the double doors that Kiora entered, and all eyes turned to her.

"We can now call this meeting to order." Max, their superior, called the room to attention, laying her eyes on the latecomer. She stood taller than most fairies, at six feet and three inches. Max's body was slim but muscular and dark as the night sky outside the tower. She had sister locks that fell to her waist and a thin unibrow that stretch across her face dyed a rainbow of colors. "Now that everyone is here."

"Sorry." Kiora apologized and took her seat.

"No apologies needed." Max nodded, and the locks shifted around her head.

"Then why mention it?" Roe muttered and rolled her eyes.

"Shh," Kiora nudged her, not wanting to call any more attention to them than was necessary.

"I know that this is an unusual meeting. Typically, we avoid having so many of you here at once, but we've received some troubling reports." Max went on. "There are problems with the wolves. Their battles with the vampires grow deadlier each day, which has pushed their fight out of their normal territories.

That means we need to be sure we watch our borders even more than we have been. For that reason, we are going to be shifting teams around."

"Um," Kiora raised her hand. "Does that mean you'll move me to a new area?"

"Is there a problem with that?" Max peered at her. It was bad enough that Kiora was late, now she questioned the superior's judgement.

"It's just that, the area I patrol I'm familiar with. I understand it." She hurried for a reason that would be good enough.

"That might work against you. If you're too familiar with an area, you get laxed." They heavy voice of Doni, a short light-skinned man who'd been a thorn in Kiora's side since she joined the guards, spoke. "You need to be on your toes for this one."

"That will not happen." Kiora snipped rolled her eyes at the unsolicited opinion.

"We will announce revised assignments at the next turn over meetings. As for now, keep your usual assigned posts." Max took control of the conversation again. "The bigger issue now is the rumor that the Alpha's son is missing. As you know, we expect the wolves to change their leadership soon. This could get really ugly and soon if they don't find him."

Kiora's heart slammed in her chest. Could the man in her hideout be the son of the alpha? He didn't look all that impressive, but she hadn't seen many wolves up close to compare him to. And what of his missing brother? That would also mean that the one he hoped to save could likely be the next alpha.

"Do we think the wolves would attack Rege again?" Doni asked, interrupting Kiora's thoughts. "Is that why things are changing?"

"Right now, there is no indication that will happen." Max answered.

"So why are we doing this?" another guard questioned.

"Because there was no sign of it happening the last time." Roe answered, and all eyes turned to her. "Think about it. The first time, when wolves started snatching up fairies, we had no issue with them before they did that. We were on good terms, as far as I know. They got desperate, and that desperation put us at risk. It happened once, and it can happen again."

"Roe is correct. And that is why we are going to be shifting our efforts until there is a resolution found." Max spoke. "Again, everyone to your posts. High alert. The morning shift is up. Night team, make sure you're fully rested."

"Before you all leave. Has anyone seen anything suspicious?" Claire, another superior who sat next to Max's side, asked the room. Her voice boomed around them, carrying the power of her short stature. Claire was a plus sized woman who could take down the largest threat with the flick of her wrist. She trained endlessly to increase her strength and stamina. All guards hoped to reach her power level, most never would.

Kiora thought about keeping her report to herself. She could hide the details about what she saw, but questioned if that would be the best thing to do. Doing so might put her people in harm's way. The reason she became a guard was so she could protect others from what happened to her sister. Keeping the incident a secret could mean putting everyone in harm, but she didn't want to give up the man. Something in her gut told her that was the wrong then to do.

"I," Kiora spoke up. She decided the best thing to do was alert them of the potential issue without telling them anything specific about the man. "I saw something that could be suspicious. Movement just outside the territory limits, but I fell. When I got up, it was gone. I'm not sure what it was, but I checked the area and I saw nothing."

"Do you think it could have been a wolf?" Claire asked, her eyes locking on Kora and searching for the truth.

"It's possible," Kiora gave just enough truth to ease suspicion. "I didn't see anything that I thought would be an immediate threat."

"Why didn't you mention this before?" Max asked, her gaze narrowing on me just like Claire's.

"Another reason we should put you somewhere else." Kiora's number one hater, Doni, interrupted.

"Doni, please keep your thoughts to yourself." Claire spoke, and the man sunk back into his seat.

"You just told us about the threat of wolves. Like I said, I saw nothing I thought we needed to be concerned about. There was no threat to my life, no evidence of violence. But now that I know we are in a heightened state, I assume you want everything reported, no matter my personal assessment of the threat."

"You're correct." Max paused looking at Kiora as she tried to determine if the guard was lying, then gave a tight nod. "Everyone, please report all details of your watches. No matter how big or small the details seem to be to you. Everything is an issue. Keep your eyes sharp."

"Everyone, you're dismissed." Claire's voice boomed and the guards quickly got up to leave the meeting hall.

Kiora watched the others leave but waited behind for a chance to talk to the one person who vouched for her when she sought to join the guard.

"Superior, Max." Kiora approached the woman and addressed her formally.

"Kiora." She turned to her, eyes kinder than before, and continued. "I know that look on your face, the slight lilt at the corner of your lips. You want something. What is it?"

"Please don't move me." Kiora spoke softly. "I know it may be a lot to ask with everything going on now, but I really think it's better if I stay where I am."

"Kiora, this is not the time." Max pinched the bridge of her nose with a deep sigh. "You know I have a soft spot for you, and I'm always on your side, but right now, I have to do what's best for the safety of our people."

"You know how much that area means to me." Kiora leaned on Max's heart strings. "It may be selfish to ask, and I know that you have a duty to our people. But I need to be there."

Max and Kiora shared a relationship that went beyond professional boundaries which Kiora believed was also the source of jealousy for people like Doni. Max wasn't just an advocate for Kiora on the guard. She was the closest thing the rookie had left to family. Max was her mother's best friend, and she took and she took Kiora and her sister under her wing after their parents both succumbed to a deadly illness. The disease swept through their home and took the lives of five thousand fairies.

It was because of their parent's demise, the threat to their health, that her sister focused her life on researching and developing cures for deadly infections and diseases. It was what inspired Kiora to join the guard after her sister's disappearance. She couldn't fathom taking up such a complex cause, but she could protect their people in another way. Max supported both girls and their endeavors. She also knew that the sisters had a special location where they would hide out together.

"Yes, and I assigned you area five because I know your connection to the land there, but you've already shown that your attention to detail is lacking. You reported in late and failed to inform us of an important detail." Max scolded her. "I cannot, in good faith, stand as the leader of the guard and let your carelessness slip by."

"I-," Kiora wanted to defend herself, but Max didn't allow it.

"Look, I get it." Max held her hand up. "Before this, you were a historian. After your sister disappeared, you showed great promise for the guard and we allowed it, but I won't give you special treatment. You've been here for less than a year and those

16

far superior to your position wouldn't dare to come to me with the request you have."

"I know. I'm not asking for you to treat me any differently than the other guards."

"Are you not?" Max tilted her head. "This sounds a lot like a request for special consideration, Kiora. I love you, but I am not blinded by that love. We will announce assignments at the next shift change. Do not be late."

"Thank you." Kiora turned to leave but paused. "Max, I can handle myself. I know you worry about me. I get that. But please trust that I will do the right thing."

"I trust you will. For now, get some rest. And take a shower. You stink."

"How'd it go?" Roe leaned against the side of the door, chewing on a piece of taffy candy. "She chew you out?"

"It went about as good as anyone would expect." Kiora held her hand out and Roe put a piece of the berry-flavored treat in her hand. "It's always so awkward when I speak to her now. Part of my brain looks at Max like a mother, but I have to remember I'm supposed to switch that part off."

"Think you're up to another awkward interaction?" Roe asked.

"You have something in mind?" Kiora looked at her friend. "Go on."

"Nothing, but a sulking ex-boyfriend might pop up."

"I hope not." Kiora shook her head. "I can't deal with him right now."

"Sucks to be you then, because here he comes." Kiora pointed toward the approaching man, then stood up straight. "I'll leave you to it, girl. I have the morning shift this week and the sun is on the rise."

"I'll check in with you later." Kiora waved as Roe opened her wings and took flight.

"Kiora." His voice was as deep as the well outside her childhood home where she first laid eyes on him.

"Marius?" Kiara addressed the man, who she still found physically appealing despite her emotional disgust. He carried himself well. Bald head, well-groomed beard, and wearing a suit tailored to his toned body. Marius wasn't a territory guard. He was a part of the outreach team, so his attire was far more formal than the others.

"Are you okay?" Marius asked. "You seemed a little off in there."

"I didn't realize you were in there, but I'm fine." Kiora brushed off his concern. "I had one bad day, and everyone is acting like I'm no longer fit for my job."

"I didn't mean to insinuate that you weren't fit, Kiora." Marius spoke with caution. "Don't get me wrong here."

"All I care about now is going home so I can rest. A lot on my mind and I'm on duty tomorrow."

"Is that why you're insisting on being in sector five?" he tilted his head. "I know you like being out there, but I don't get why you refuse to be moved."

"Is that any of your business?" Kiara pointed over her shoulder at the door to the tower. "Last I checked, the superiors were the only ones who had anything to do with sector assignments. Besides, your job is out in the world, not here. Why are you here now?"

"Kiora, I'm just trying to look out for you." Marius started in on the same song of protection she'd heard too many times before.

"That's not your job anymore Marius. Remember? We aren't together anymore." Kiora reminded him of their relationship status. "You can let it go. I'm more than capable of looking out for myself."

"Are you ever going to stop hating me?" Marius asked. "I only did what I thought was right, Kiora."

"I don't hate you. I never hated you. You did what you thought was right, and that decision disappointed me. You didn't believe in me. You didn't trust in my instincts or allow me to advocate for myself. That hurt me, Marius. Will that ever go away? I doubt it."

Kiora admitted to him what she hadn't been able to put into words without going off on him. When she pleaded for the guards to let her go look for her sister, she expected him to agree. She thought he would offer to escort her. Instead, he sided with the others. Said it was too risky, and that she wasn't in the right mind to go. It didn't matter if he was right. She expected the man she loved, the man who claimed to love her more than anything else, to stand by her side and support her choices.

She almost forgave him, told herself that he was just concerned for her safety. Until she overheard him talking to Max.

"I'm sorry, but something is wrong with Kiora. She's fixated on this and won't let it go. If you let her go out, there, it will hurt her and likely whoever is with her." Kiora recalled the conversation. Marius stood in the meeting room with Max, unknowing that Kiora stood outside the door listening in.

"I expected you to be the one to volunteer to join her." Max stood at the bench looking down at him.

"Superior Max," Marius continued. *"You know I love Kiora, but I cannot overlook the obvious issue in her logic right now. I hate to be harsh, but do you honestly think Safir is still out there?"*

"No, I don't but Kiora needs to come to that understanding for herself." Max justified. *"We can't force it to happen."*

"So let her come to that understanding here, where she is safe. Letting her go out there only puts her at risk. Do you really want to lose her, too?"

"You don't think she's capable of handling herself out there?" Max asked.

"No, I honestly do not." Marius spoke the words she believed sealed Max's decision to vote against Kiora.

Kiora couldn't stand to be around him after that. Every time she looked at him, she heard his words again. She felt his lack of faith and couldn't get it out of her head. She also couldn't trust the man who went behind her back to work against her.

"I'll do whatever I can to fix that." Marius said. "Just give me a chance."

"I really wish you would drop it. I don't trust you Marius. You didn't believe in me then. There's no reason for me to believe that would ever change." Kiora turned her back to him. "I'm going home now. I need to shower."

"I wasn't going to say it." He tried for a soft joke.

"Then don't." Kiora snapped, then took flight, headed home.

Three

Kiora considered returning to her hideout to check on the injured wolf but realized it would raise too much suspicion. No one ever went to check a guard post if they weren't on duty. She knew Marius would look after her for the night even if he didn't specifically say it. Anytime the man approached her, she could feel his presence with her for at least a day after because of the other guards who worked with him.

Even if Marius couldn't be there, someone would watch and report back. If he thought even for a moment that she was acting strange, he wouldn't waste a moment before he ran to Max again. That wasn't something she could risk.

Instead, she went home to the little house built for her by her father before he died. On their property were three houses. The main house and the largest was where her parents stayed. The two others were smaller and meant for her and her sister.

Even after their death, she couldn't bring herself to move into the main house. It felt wrong.

But the property belonged to her, so no one else questioned her or tried to take it away. Max and Roe both suggested she move, but there was nowhere in Rege that felt right. Kiora joked that if she ever left her home, she'd be leaving the city altogether.

Her house was like most of the others in the city. Structured by nature, built only from the materials provided by the earth, and reinforced with their own magic. The roof was a living platform overgrown with various wildflowers, unlike the moss that covered her sister's roof.

Fairies drew their power from the nature around them. They tapped into the strength of the earth and manipulated the elements. Because their powers were a gift from nature, they lived a life that showed the most respect they could for the gifts provided. While some people carved their homes inside of massive trees, others lived in underground structures, much like the hideout where she hid the wolf.

Inside her home was a simple interior. One bedroom, one bathroom, a large kitchen and an open space that doubled as a sitting and a dining area. It was enough space for her, and she wanted nothing more. Not if it meant leaving her home.

As always, when she crossed the threshold, she undressed. She hated the idea of tracking anything into her home from the woods. After having spent time with the wolf; she didn't want the smell that everyone else picked up to linger and stink up the place.

In her underwear she crossed the room to the mantle above the fireplace where a single lavender candle sat next to the picture of her family. She lit the candle, blew her family a kiss, and then headed to the bathroom. Just inside the bathroom door was a full-length mirror. At one time it was where she did outfit checks with her sister. With little reason for her to dress up, its purpose became only to reveal any injuries she may have sustained.

Kiora wasn't the best on her feet, which is why no one questioned her when she said she fell on her ass resulting in the unsavory odor. She liked to blame it on her full figure curves and would say her ass threw her off balance. Time and time again, she would come home to new bruises or cuts that she had to tend to before her next shift. Upon inspection, she found no bruises, but she couldn't take her eyes off her reflection.

Kiora wondered how long it had been since she'd really looked at herself for more than the adjustment of her appearance before running out the door. Her body was changing. In every sense, she was still young, but there was a maturity happening there that she hadn't paid attention to.

Her hips widened, signaling that she was physically ready to produce new life. Her breasts were still perky, but they felt heavier, fuller than before. There was more muscle tone in her arms, torso and legs, the result of her training. Unlike the other guards, she spent three hours before each shift sharpening her skills. If she wanted them to take her seriously, she would have to step up her game. Because if the question ever came for her to leave their home to protect their people, she didn't want there to be concern about her abilities.

She turned from her reflection and the critique of her body and continued her routine. The heat from the shower transformed the bathroom into a steam room, and she stepped into the flow of water, welcoming the instant feeling of relaxation it provided. She remained under the flow longer than usual, as there was a lot more on her mind to be considered.

When she got out of the shower, she took the bun out of her hair and let the braids flow down her back. Tucked inside the bun were the gold tips of her braids. The gold foils wrapped around the ends were her sister's signature look. Adding them to her hair was another way she felt she could keep her memory alive. She wrapped her hair to protect it when she slept and then headed for the kitchen.

Though she wasn't hungry, she forced herself to eat because she knew she needed the nutrients, especially after all the energy she spent moving the wolf. She prepared her meals for the next day and made extra because she would take some with her on her watch, not for herself but for the wolf. It wouldn't be suspicious most people carried food and other snacks with them.

Kiora typically opted out of this, but occasionally she would do the same. With her food prepped, her body clean and her mind heavy, Kiora went to bed. She expected her mind to be flooded with thoughts about her sister, but all she could think about was the man that she left in their hideout.

The next evening, after her training, she packed her things and made it back to the meeting room before anyone else arrived.

"Trying to make a good impression?" Doni strolled in with a cocky grin pasted on his face.

"Whatever, get the stick out of your ass already." Roe followed him. "I swear it's like you're in love with Kiora. Why else would you keep bugging her?"

Claire entered, interrupting whatever witty comeback Doni may have come up with. Kiora waited for Max to enter the room after her, but she never did. As the rest of the guards arrived, Max was still missing. Claire started the meeting, calling everyone to attention and handed out their new orders. Kiora held her breath hoping to find relief when Claire called out her assignment.

"Sector five, Kiora will maintain." Claire announced.

Kiora nodded but kept her show of relief at a minimum. Anything too dramatic, like the enormous sigh and energetic clapping she wanted to do, would have had everyone questioning her about why the hell she cared so much.

"Of course, you get to keep your precious area." Doni muttered. "Must be nice to have the superior in your back pocket."

"You want to say that again?" Claire's voice boomed, and the room fell silent. "Are you questioning our judgement, Doni?"

"No. Sorry." Doni choked on his words. Regardless of how he felt, it wasn't appropriate to speak negatively about the superiors, especially with one standing right in front of him.

"I didn't think so. You all have your orders. Get to work." Claire said, then left the room.

Kiora looked at Doni, expecting him to say something else, but he stood and silently left the room.

"Max really likes you." Roe nudged Kiora as the two women headed out the meeting hall.

"For now." Kiora sucked her teeth.

"Why would you say that?" Roe yawned. "You think that's going to change any time soon?"

"I just get the feeling the more I go against what she wants, the less she'll like me." Kiora admitted. "I've been the good one for so long. Doing whatever I could to make sure that I didn't cause too much of a fuss for her."

"Planning on a rebellion?" Roe stopped her. "Who are we fighting?"

"No one." Kiora laughed. "It's not like I'm out here looking for trouble, but I want to go my own way. Do my own thing. And eventually it's going to come to a point when what I want doesn't align with what she wants."

"Well, I'm glad that it's not down to us fighting, because I need to sleep." Kiora stretched her hands over her head with another big yawn. "So be good on your watch, please. I'll see you later."

"Bye." Kiora waved at the woman who left her standing outside the tower with her new orders.

Kiora stood there alone for a moment and allowed herself to feel the relief that she hid when it was announced that she could keep her area. Keeping the area didn't mean she was completely out of the woods. The person responsible for the sector during the day could stumble across her hideout, but it had yet to happen in the six months she'd been assigned her post. Also, as long as she could visit the area, she could reinforce her barrier at the end of her shift.

Kiora performed her duties as usual. She checked the report from the previous watch and found that Ash, the woman with gray wings, had found nothing unusual. Another relief. After getting her brief, she headed out.

Kiora checked her area, completing her same pattern as always. Nothing could be off. She maintained a higher sense of awareness because she knew others would watch her. She could feel their eyes on her. And it was four hours into her watch when the spies left her, surely heading back to report to her ex about how uneventful her night was.

She was on the ground. Others took aerial positions. But she knew how to hide from them. They coasted overhead twice every hour. But the increase in their security detail meant that they were increasing the number of times that they covered the route.

When she had an opening, she returned to the hideout worried the wolf might not be there, but he was.

Stretched across the cot, legs hanging off the end, and snoring like a full-grown bear. Kiora put down the food and water she'd packed for him near his feet. Again, her brain when into historian mode as she examined him. Most of the superficial wounds healed but a cake of dirt and blood still covered his naked body.

Feeling strange about sitting in the space with an unconscious and naked man, Kiora dug through the chests at the back of the hideout and found a blanket to cover him with. There were also clothes but nothing that would fit him. She considered going to find something but realized that collecting clothing for the man would have people questioning her.

Just as the fuzzy pink fabric covered in embroidered roses touched him, he stirred, swiping at the air to the left of him and muttering something about vampires. She quickly backed away and sat close to the entrance where she could escape easily if he woke up swinging or shifting back to his wolf.

It took another hour for the wolf to wake. In that time, she'd done two more sweeps of her territory. Knowing that she had a secret to protect, Kiora couldn't slack on her responsibilities. Which meant she could only spend ten to fifteen minutes at a time with the wolf.

It was almost time for her to go on another sweep when he groaned.

"You're alive." Kiora said as his eyes opened and immediately regretted it.

He jumped from the cot, swiftly moved across the space, and his large hand wrapped around her throat to cut off her air. She wrapped her hands around his wrist and struggled beneath his strength. Her vision blurred and all she could think was that this man, the one she saved, was going to kill her.

Kiora slapped her hand against the wall of the hideout and seven vines shot out and wrapped around him. The thick lines wrapped around his legs, arms, and torso and pulled him away from her. He fought against them, but they strapped him against the opposite wall.

"Thank you," Kiora said to the vines between gasps for air. She placed her hand over her throat. "Dammit."

"What is this?" He growled as he struggled against the vines. His muscles expanded in his arm, veins bulging until one vine broke, but another quickly replaced it. "Who are you? What do you want from me?"

"I don't want anything from you, asshole." Kiora snapped. "I can't believe I put myself at risk of losing my damn job trying to help you, only for you to wake up and attack me!"

"Help me?" He shook his head. "What are you talking about? Where am I?"

"You're in Rege, or at least you're on the border."

"What? How the hell did I get here?" The man questioned and shook his head from the disorientation.

"I don't know, but I found you near death and exposed. I brought you here because my dumbass actually felt sorry for you. Maybe I should have left you there to rot or reported you to the superiors." She pointed to the exit. "You aren't supposed to be here. You realize that, right?"

"I don't remember coming here."

"What reason do I have to lie to you about that?" Kiora scoffed at the insinuation.

"No, I can tell that you're not. I'm sorry." He paused and narrowed his gaze at her. "What do you want from me?"

"Seriously?" Kiora laughed dryly. "You're beaten and bloodied. I brought you to safety and gave you food and water. What's wrong with you? You know the decent thing to say right now is thank you. Instead, you're here accusing me of something."

"Where is my brother?" he ignored her comment, his brain only focused on gathering information. He pulled from the vines again, this time snapping two of them. Instead of using vines to restrain him, she called to the dirt behind it.

"What the fuck!" he yelled as the dirt split and the vines pulled him into the opening before the dirt slammed shut around him. Leaving only his head exposed.

"Look, I don't know you or your brother." She placed her palm against the wall and thanked the earth for its help. "If you try that again, I will kill you."

"Dammit. I was supposed to keep him safe." He dropped his head. "I failed."

"Your brother? What happened to you?" When he didn't answer, Kiora stepped closer to him. "Look, I'm trying to help you, but I can't do that if you're just going to keep attacking me and ignoring my questions. Do you really think I'm going to free you if I think you'll hurt me?"

"They attacked us. Vampires. Dammit." His voice broke with his remorse. "Killed seven men before they made it to us. I told him to run, to get away, but I don't know if he did. I tried to lead them away from him. They were supposed to follow me, not him. I don't even remember coming this way. We were at least fifty miles north of your border."

"You ran fifty miles, and you don't remember doing it?"

"Apparently." He shrugged. "Easy to do in my wolf form. Which I assume I was in, considering I'm naked now."

His eyes dropped to his body, which was currently covered by a wall of dirt. Kiora averted her eyes as if she could see through the thick barrier.

"What's your name?" she changed the subject.

"What?" he tilted his head. "You don't know?"

"If I did, I wouldn't ask." She shrugged. "Look, if I'm going to help you, I should know who you are. Might make the risk I'm taking worth it."

"Raden, my name is Raden." He answered with hesitation.

"Raden," Kiora's heart caught in her throat. "As in, son to the Alpha, Raden?"

"Yes, and my brother is Roden. The next in line to be alpha. He's missing."

"Fuck." Kiora dropped to the floor and crossed her legs beneath her. "Of course, I dragged the Alpha's son into my damn hideout. How could I be so stupid? Wait. If what you say is true, you will have the mark, right?"

She stood. And crossed over to the wall where she trapped him. Palm to the dirt, she asked it to part so she could see his chest. The dirt and blood covered the dark skin. She grabbed the water she brought for him to drink and poured it on his chest, using her hand to wipe away the mess. With his skin clear, the tattoo, the mark of the Alpha's bloodline, stood was perfectly clear. A crescent moon with four strikes through it signifying the claw marks of the wolf.

"It's true." She whispered and placed her hand over her mouth. "You're the damn Alpha's son!"

"I am. Now, I need to get out of here. I have to find my brother."

"I hate to break it to you, but you're in no condition to do that." Kiora held her hand up, hesitating to ask the dirt to move. "I'm going to let you go. Please don't attack me again."

Raden nodded, and Kiora hesitated to trust him but asked the dirt and vines to free him.

"Thank you for helping me, but I have to go now." Raden darted for the exit, attempting to outrun the woman, but collapsed on the ground. His body rippled with chaotic energy and the sound of cracking bones filled the small space. Kiora covered her gasp as she watched his body struggle before he hit the floor. "Dammit! I can't shift. My ribs."

"Good." Kiora dropped her hand to her side as she watched the man's continued suffering. "Not to be mean about it, but because of the shit going on with you and the vampires, they've bulked up the patrols here. If you go out there right now, they will catch you, and I'm sure you know what that means."

"A violation of the treaty." Raden punched the floor, leaving the impression of his fist in the dirt. "What the hell am I supposed to do now? My brother needs me."

"I can help." Kiora kneeled in front of him. "I'm a guard. Just give me one more day. You can heal, and I'll talk to my superior and come up with a plan."

"Yeah, right, they'll kill me," Raden said. "Or at the very least, capture me and use me as a bargaining chip."

"That's not what we're about. You know that." Kiora defended her people.

"You severed our connection with the moon and our magic." Raden snorted. "Like I'd put it past you to want to use me as leverage to get what you want."

"Because you were murdering us!" Kiora stuck her finger in his face and when he growled at her, baring his teeth, she held firm. "Put your damn teeth away. How dare you sit here and say that as if we were the ones to come into your homes and steal your people? Look, I'm trying to help you, but if you want to pull this shit, I will leave you here to rot. I know our peoples' histories and yours is the one covered in blood, not mine."

"You're right," Raden pulled back. "I apologize."

"Now, there is one I trust with my life." Kiora continued with her plan to help him. "She's like a mother to me. She will help us figure this out."

"Why should I trust your opinion of this woman?" he laughed. "If you trusted her so much, why doesn't she already know I'm here?"

"You're right." Kiora sighed. "I could have turned you in last night, you know. But I didn't. I brought you here."

"Why did you bring me here?" he asked. "You said you're a guard. I'm assuming you have strict directives about announced guests. Especially ones you find bloodied and beaten."

Kiora thought about his question and looked at the man in front of her. His question was valid, and she had an answer for it, but she didn't want to tell him. Even while looking into his dark eyes that made her stomach tighten, she knew that to tell him how she felt about her history and her sister would mean putting herself in a more vulnerable position than she was prepared for.

"That's not important right now." She refused to answer his question and instead refocused their conversation. "What is important is that you drink the water and eat the soup. It will aid in your healing. How long does it usually take?"

"What?"

"Your body, to heal. You were pretty beat up. You still look bad now, but not nearly as bad as yesterday." She looked at his chest. "But your bones haven't finished healing. That's why you couldn't shift just now. Right?"

"Yes. Healing time depends on the severity of the injuries. Those vampires did a number on me." He touched his side. "It shouldn't take much longer, but it's still more time than I would prefer."

"But you got away," Kiora said. "Vampires attacked, and you made it out alive."

"I did." He sighed. "Just wish I knew if Roden got away or not."

"Rumor is that he's missing." She revealed what Max told the guards. "It's why we're all on high alert now. Look, I'll figure this out. You can't stay here much longer."

"I know." Raden looked at her with a calculating expression. "You trust your superior?"

"I do, why?" She asked.

"Do you think they would allow you to accompany me when I leave?" his question shocked her.

"Excuse me?" she gasped. This man knew nothing about her, accused her of attacking him, but expected her to run off with him after he just said vampires were out to kill him.

"I'm healing, but I'm not strong enough to fight on my own. If I stay here another day, it still won't be enough. I could go back home and recruit help, but that would mean losing a lot of time."

"You just tried to kill me three seconds ago and questioned if I was trustworthy. Now you want me to run off with you to face vampires? Why do you trust me all of a sudden?"

"I don't, but I need help." he looked her up and down. "You're not the biggest, but I can tell you're strong and what you did with the vines and earth, your skills can come in handy in a battle against vampires."

"Are you crazy? It's bad enough I'm doing it here." She sighed. Max might allow him safe passage out, but it wouldn't mean she would be okay with Kiora running off with him. "Even if my superior would let me help you after finding out

I hid the fact that you were here, I'm going to take a lot of shit for this."

"I understand." Raden dropped the issue easily.

"Are you really close to your brother?" Though he didn't press her about her decision, Kiora's mind was already trying to figure out a reason to help him.

"What?" he looked at her. "Why are you asking me this?"

"You prayed for his safety just before you passed out. I assumed that meant you and your brother were close."

"He's my best friend." Raden's shoulders dropped, and he sighed. "We've been inseparable our entire lives. And I was supposed to protect him. I messed up and I want to make it right. I have to."

"Dammit." Kiora paced the floor, hands on her hips, and muttered to herself. "This is really stupid, Kiora. You know it. You're going to end up dead because of your dumbass sentiment."

"I'm sorry, what?" Raden frowned. "Are you okay?"

"Max is going to kick my ass for even asking this." She pointed to him. "I told myself I would help you heal, and then send you on your way. That's it."

"I'm confused." He laughed at her. "What is happening here?"

"I'll be back tomorrow." She pointed to the provisions she brought for him. "Eat, drink, rest. Hopefully, I return with good news and clothing."

Four

Kiora completed her duties as usual. The interaction with Raden lasted longer than she planned, which put her three minutes behind for the last patrol of her sector, but she didn't think that anyone would notice. She no longer felt the eyes of Marius or his men on her. Which meant whatever initial reports they'd given him satisfied his obsession with his ex.

As she flew above the trees and headed back to the tower, she went over what she wanted to say to Max at least twenty times. This was something she had to do and typically Max was supportive whenever she felt that way, but this was different. What she wanted would put not only herself, but her people at risk if things went wrong. She wondered how the woman who practically raised her would feel about her request to run off with the werewolf and potentially go head-to-head with vampires.

By the time she reached the tower, Kiora decided the best way to approach the topic with Max would be to talk about it from a strategic standpoint. She had to keep any evidence of her emotions out of it because Max would not go for anything she thought was based on an errant feeling. Especially when it touched on the grief she had about her sister.

The problem was, Kiora was having a hard time deciding what their strategy would be. And then she thought about what Raden said. There was an opportunity for them in this situation, one that could better the position of the fairies in the world. They had a treaty with the wolves, yes, but this was an opportunity to turn a treaty into an allyship.

She landed outside the tower with the others. She wasn't early, but at least she wasn't late and wouldn't get chewed out again. Inside, she sat in her usual seat next to her friend, but remained quiet as her thoughts continued on the path of strategy. Doni made another crude remark about her favor from Max, but Kiora had too much on her mind to give him the attention he so obviously wanted.

Claire entered the room, this time accompanied by Lokus, another superior who had bright green hair and earrings that hung down to his waist. Lokus only attended meetings when they could find no one else to be there, which meant something was wrong. Kiora's mind shifted between worrying about the wolf and a newfound concern. Max. Where was she, and why did she send Lokus in her place?

After the meeting was done, and everyone left the meeting hall, Kiora stayed behind. She sat alone, listening to the echoes of her own thoughts before she worked up the nerve to find Max. There was no way she could let another day pass without speaking to the woman, despite how much she dreaded the conversation. Raden wouldn't wait that long. Besides, nothing promised Max would show the next day. If something was wrong, it could keep the superior away for a while.

She knew where she could find Max. In the superior quarters in the towers. The first floor of the building was the meeting room, where the guards took their orders. The second and third floors held offices where they conducted meetings of greater importance, typically between superiors and other guardian types like Marius.

The fourth and fifth floors were recreational areas for the superiors who lived in the tower. Complete with fitness arenas, a spa, and a lounge area. The top five floors were the homes of the superiors. Max's home was on the ninth floor.

There were three ways to climb the tower, stairs, the elevator, or through the central shaft. Kiora chose the shaft. It meant using her wings and eliminated any chance for awkward small talk should she run into anyone. She passed one person, a man who looked more uninterested in idle talk than she was. As she exited the shaft on the ninth floor, she gave herself a pep talk.

"You can do this, girl. Max is reasonable. She will understand as long as you present the facts, logically. Don't go in there and lose your nerve." Her words ended as she stood at the door to Max's home. Two minutes later, she finally knocked on the door.

"Come in, Kiora." Max called from the other side of the door.

"How did you know it was me?" Kiora entered the home and closed the door behind her. She found Max sitting in the middle of a large living room wrapped in a black robe.

"Really?" She pointed to the wall of screens. On each one was a different view of areas both inside and outside the tower.

"When the hell did you put these in?" Kiora peered at the screens and her heart stopped when she realized there was footage of the borders. Had Max seen her? Did she already know what Kiora was there to confess?

"About eight months ago. You'd know, but you don't visit me here anymore." Max narrowed her gaze.

"Right." Kiora said nervously.

"What have you done?" Max asked.

"Why do you assume I've done something?" Kiora clutched her chest in feigned shock.

"Kira, don't stand in my home and act like I don't know you." Max adjusted the robe around her shoulders. "You only come to visit me here when it's something big. Any other time, you would send a message for me to meet you somewhere else."

"Yeah, well, this room reminds me of some pretty tough times." Kiora looked around the room painted a soft gray with gold accents.

"When your parents died." Max nodded. "You spent a lot of time here."

"And Safir." Kiora spoke of her sister. "She loved your home. Spent more time here than I ever did."

"Yes. She did. She helped me decorate most of it." Max's laughter turned into an ugly cough, and she reached for a cup on the table nearby.

"What's wrong?" Kiora asked, smelling the aromatic scent of mint from the cup. Max hated mint, so if she was drinking it without being forced, something was wrong. "You don't look good."

"I don't feel it either." Max cleared her throat. "Definitely seen better days."

Kiora looked at the woman and finally saw it. Dark circles under her eyes, her dark-skinned looked ashen, and there was a sickly yellow tent to her eyes.

"What happened?" Kiora crossed the room to sit next to Max. "You were fine the other day."

"This sickness sets in fast." Max cleared her throat. "There are a few others who have it. We've quietly moved them into quarantine."

"Should I be here? Is it safe?" Kiora's eyes widened. "I didn't know anything about a sickness."

"And few people know about it. It's not exactly something that we have publicized, especially because it wasn't affecting our people, but it seems this virus has mutated. I was helping with moving the others when someone spit up blood and it landed right in my eye."

"Wait, it's not the same one that Safir was researching, is it?"

"Yes, it is." Max relaxed into the black couch where she sat. "To think, we felt so relieved. We just stopped looking for a solution for this shit."

"Damn it and now it's hurting fairies too?" Kiora's stomach turned.

"Yes, and unfortunately, the only people who were even close to coming up with the cure were the wolves. Apparently, the alpha's son is a genius, and he was on his way to a new laboratory to test a cure. That's when he and his brother were attacked, and no one's heard from him since. They say their brothers have a bond that they can fill each other. You know they understand what each other need. If only we knew where the other brother was."

"What if we knew where he was?" Kiora asked the leading question and Max looked at her with sideways suspicion.

"Then we could ask him to find his brother and potentially the cure for this. Apparently, the wolves have lifelines for the important members of their societies. Their like trackers attacked to the person's heartbeat. It's a way that they can tell if a wolf has fallen. Both brothers' lifelines are still active, though one is weaker than the other."

"If I were to stumble across the brother and he were to ask me to join him on the search for his missing brother, what would you say about that?"

"Are we speaking hypothetically right now?" Max sucked her teeth.

"Let's just say we are." Kiora shrugged.

"First, I would ask you why you hadn't reported this after your duty. I'd have to consider that this is something you were hiding for a while." Max took a deep breath as her eyes locked on Kiora's face. "Then I would ask you what you plan to do when you potentially come up against vampires, because that is who was after them. The vampires don't want the wolves to come up with a cure. The humans are their primary food source, and they are unaffected by this.

As far as the vampires are concerned, the wolves are getting hit hardest. It makes sense to let the virus continue to spread. So, no matter where those brothers go, there is a huge target on their backs. Is that something you really want to get involved with?"

"If it means potentially saving hundreds, if not thousands, of people, then yes. Would you not if you were in my position?"

"In your position? I thought we were speaking hypothetically, Kiora. Is there something that you need to tell me?"

"Yes." Kiora lifted her chin and straightened her shoulders. The action was for nothing more than to give her the courage to admit what she'd hidden. "I found him."

"Found who exactly?" Max knew what she meant but of course would make her say the words.

"Raden, one of the alpha sons. He was hurt when I found him, and I took him to our hideout, you know, the one Safir and I had at the border's edge. He's there now healing, and he may or may not have asked me to join him in the hunt for his brother."

"You have got to be kidding me right now with this. After everything I've done for you, why would you hide this from me, Kiora? Do you know what this could mean if the wolves were to find that you have their son locked up in a dungeon? Do you know how bad that looks?"

"That wasn't my intention. When I found him, he was on the brink of death." Kiora explained herself and swallowed the lump of nerves that formed in her throat. "He had been through a fight with vampires. I wanted to help him. If I left him where I found him, he would have died. And I didn't know who he was when I found him, Max. I just thought I was doing the right thing."

"There's something else you aren't telling me, Kiora." Max pointed at her and narrowed her eyes. "Even if you wanted to help him, you would have come to me. What aren't you saying?"

"He was praying for his brother. He asked the goddess to protect him the way he couldn't. Maybe it's my fault for being sentimental, but it got me thinking about Safir and how I wished I could have been there for her and how no one would allow me to." She held back her tears because they wouldn't help her in her conversation with Max. "If I told you about it, you would have snatched him up and sent him back to the wolves. I just wanted to give him a fighting chance to help his brother. But now he needs my help. That's why I came here."

"You came here to ask my permission to run off with the son of the alpha?" Max's dry laughed turned into a painful cough.

"You say that as if I'm running off for some fling. It's a mission one that might help us not that it's the reason I'm doing it." Kiora gestured toward the cup of tea, but Max waved it off.

"How? How do you see this benefitting us?" She challenged. "Make your case."

"Well, you said they're working on a cure. Obviously, you're sick and others will be too. I think they would prioritize the fairies if we help them find the one who can make the cure. Also, the wolves and the fairies have been at each other's neck for so long and for what reason?" Kiora stood and paced the room as she gave voice to her racing thoughts.

"We have this treaty, but maybe that's not enough. The vampires are getting bolder and more aggressive than they have ever been. How long do you think it's gonna be before they come after us? They're already reports of the vampires going into new territories. This problem is bigger. We could make the wolves our allies hell, maybe work with other people and take care of this problem before it gets any worse. The vampires will let the entire world suffer with this disease just so that they can take out the werewolves. Do you think it's gonna end there, really?"

"It sounds like you really thought this through." Max smiled. "You've laid out a logical case."

"I have. And I know that it's a long shot, but this could be a way to bridge the relationship." Kiora offered more reason.

"You do this, and no one else knows about it." Max pointed a long finger at Kiora. "If you fail, that's on you."

"I understand that, and I wouldn't have it any other way. Just give me a chance. I don't know why, but I trust him, and he needs my help." Kiora's mood lifted with Max's lean towards approval.

"What do you need?" Max asked.

"To start with some clothes for the man." Kiora laughed. "Their clothes don't shift with them and right now he's... well, he's naked. I have things, but nothing that's gonna fit him. I thought about getting some stuff from dad, but he's a way bigger than my father ever was."

"What about backup, Kiora?" Max sighed, unconcerned with the state of Raden's attire. "I know you don't plan on doing this alone."

"I know I'll need some, but if you don't mind, I think I'd like to recruit my own. There are people here who have other intentions and report my every action to Marius and if he gets wind of this, it won't end well."

"I understand. He was not happy with me for letting me stay out there." She laughed. "He wanted me to pull you back and stick you on some desk job here until things clear up with the wolves."

"You know he has his friends stalking me now?" Kiora admitted the secret she kept from Max. "I pretend I don't notice because it's just easier that way, but this is getting ridiculous. I didn't want to say anything because it would only cause more drama. My presence already irritates some of the other guards. But Max. I don't want to be with him. I can't be with him and no matter how I expressed it, he doesn't get it. I can't let that impede this."

"Alright well, you have my blessing." Max eyed the cup of tea and frowned. "That's all I'm gonna say. Anything you need, you take. Just know that you will be under heat when you get back here, especially if you fail."

"Thank you, Max."

"Yeah, yeah." Max coughed. "And we'll deal with that crooked ex of yours when you're back."

Five

"Kiora." The voice called out to her the moment she stepped outside the tower, and she rolled her eyes.

"Dammit." she muttered, then turned to the man she wanted to avoid. "What is it Marius?"

"Are you okay?" He asked, again showing concern she didn't want.

"I'm fine." She gave him a short answer before turning to walk away.

"Kiora." He called her name again. "Stop."

"What?" she snapped. "What do you want?"

"I just wanted to talk to you." He raised his hands in peace. "You don't have to be so mean to me, you know."

"About what Marius? What more is there to say? Is it about work? If not, I don't want to hear it." She stood her ground.

Marius was becoming more annoying as time went on and being nice wasn't getting her point across.

"You really care so little for me now?" he pouted.

"I just want to be left alone. If you cared for me as much as you claim to, then you would do that." She said, unaffected by the puppy dog eyes he gave her. "Instead, you pester me, stalk me, and have your minions watching my every move. What are you even doing here now? Why are you always here? Isn't there some convoy you should be with right now? Isn't that your job?"

"Fine, I'll leave you alone." He stepped back. "I wish I understood why you feel like this about me now. But if you want me gone, I'm gone."

"Yeah right." She shook her head, turned, and walked away. It wasn't the first time he'd promised to give her the space she asked for.

Kiora wanted to go straight to Roe to set things up, but she knew that even though Marius said he would leave her alone, he wouldn't. That was the way it always went, pretend to give her space, and then encroach on it again and again. Two minutes after she left him, she felt the eyes of his snitches on her.

So instead of making the preparations for what would be a near impossible task, she went home. She undressed at the door, lit the candle by her family's picture, and then headed to take her shower. She ate her meal and when her dishes hit the sink that she finally felt the eyes of his men fall away from her.

Kiora made herself a promise that she wouldn't allow him to stalk her any longer. She would have to talk to Max or one of the other superiors about Marius's abuse of power, but that was not the time. She had more important things to worry about than a creepy ex-boyfriend.

When the coast was clear, she snuck out of her house like a child breaking curfew and headed for the border. Roe handled sector three one of the more difficult areas because of the complex terrain, but she was far more skilled in her job than most of the other guards. When Kiora arrived, she announced herself because sneaking up on her friend was a bad idea.

"What the hell are you doing out here?" Roe landed in front of Kiora, perfectly balanced on a large slab of rock.

"I'm here to ask a favor." Kiora watched her friend in awe. "One that you're probably going to want to say no to."

"Is this the stuff you were talking about before? Your rebellion?" Roe asked, intrigued by the mystery. "Is this why you said Max is no longer gonna be your friend?"

"Possibly, except I spoke to Max and, well, she's giving me her blessing, though no one else is supposed to know that." Kiora nodded. "So top secret job here."

"Sounds dangerous." Roe clapped her hands. "Finally, something interest. What's up?"

"Do you remember when Max told us about how the werewolves might be a threat because the Alpha's son is missing?"

"Yes? So what?" Roe sat down on the slab she had previously stood on.

"Well, it's actually two of his sons, and I know where one of them is." Kiora paused while Roe's jaw fell open. "Actually, I may have hidden him in my hideout. The one that Safir and I built together."

"You've got to be shitting me." Roe laughed. "No wonder you've been acting so damn weird the last couple of days."

"I wish I were, but no, I'm being honest. I found him on the border's edge, beat up after an attack by the vampires. The man ran fifty miles from where he they attacked him and landed on our footstep. I didn't know who he was when I found him, but I felt like I had to help him, Roe." Kiora fought the urge to pace as she continued her story. "He was on the brink of death. I've never seen a wolf look like that before, not that I've had many encounters with wolves. His body is healing, but slower than I think it should be. So, I helped, and I put him in our hideout, and it just turned out that he is Raden."

"Raden. As in second eldest to the alpha. Damn girl, you really know how to pick a winner don't you?" She shook her head, then looked up at the cloudy sky. "What do you need from me? I know you didn't come here just to confess this secret."

"You're right. Here's the deal." Kiora squatted in front of Roe. "He needs help to find his brother. If he goes home, he'll lose too much time. We can't send communication to the werewolves because it could be dangerous if the vampires intercept the message. Right now, for all anybody knows, he's dead, and that works to our advantage. I have requested permission to help him find his brother."

"And Max said yes to this?" Roe knew exactly who Kiora went to.

"There are some greater things at stake. Max is sick and a lot of other people are gonna get sick. Raden's brother is the only person who has come anywhere near a solution for whatever this disease is. I'm hoping that by helping Raden find his brother, they can finish the cure and save Max and anyone else who may be affected."

"Well damn, this just keeps getting heavier, doesn't it?" Roe looked up at Kiora. "I thought you were going to tell me you needed me to cover your ass while you had a dirty little booty call."

"That would be a lot simpler, but no. I need your help, Roe. I can't do this on my own. I'm taking an enormous risk going out there and I need to know that I have someone I can trust in my corner." Kiora said.

"You know I got your back, Kiora. What do you need?"

"Are you sure you want to help with this?" Kiora gave her friend a chance to sit out of the drama. If they got caught, Roe would be in just as much trouble as Kiora.

"Come on girl, it's you and its Max. You guys are like my family. Shoot, you know I can't stand the one I was born into. How could I ever say no?"

"Thank you." Kiora relaxed.

"Thank me when we survive this. Tell me what you need."

"I need you to talk to Sky and Marley. If at some point we need backup, I want it to be people I trust. They need to be on point, but no one else can know about this. Don't tell them exactly what we're doing until it's necessary. Just tell them to be ready and don't even tell them it's coming from me because you-know-who is all up in my business. We won't be able to use our comms." She held up her wrist where the marks of the implanted communication devices were.

"I don't know how, but I'm pretty sure he's tapped into mine, so we're gonna have to do the braid link. When I need to talk to you, I will contact you. If I don't reach out, do not reach out to me. It has to be a one-way communication. I know that there are people listening those same people want to stop us from doing what we need to do."

"You saw him again, didn't you?" Roe started unbraiding one of her braids. "Marius. Is that why you're so paranoid?"

"Yes, and my paranoia is valid." Kiora also unraveled one of her braids. "He was waiting for me when I left Max's home. I don't understand why he won't move on. People break up all the time. What is the difference here?"

"The difference is you broke up, and he was very much not done with the relationship." Roe said. "That man fully planned to spend the rest of his life with you, Kiora."

"It's been over a year, Roe. How long am I supposed to sit here and pretend like the shit isn't creepy? It's obsessive."

"I say when you get back here, you file a report against him. I get being protective and all. At first, I thought it was sweet that he was so worried about you, but you're right. What he's doing now is over the top and I don't understand how anyone has allowed it to go on this far, especially Max."

"Max has bigger things to worry about. Besides, I never told her or anyone else about it, but she sees it just like you do. Right now, I can't deal with that. I have to focus on the task at hand, and that is helping Raden."

"Is he cute?" Roe winked.

"What?" Kiora stopped unbraiding her hair and pulled a small knife from her pocket.

"The wolf man. I mean, he gotta be cute, right? He is the alpha's son. And that man is fine. I've seen pictures of him... delicious. If his son looks anything like him, girl, no wonder you're running off to save him."

"You know that's not what this is about." Kiora cut the bottom of her unraveled braid, then handed the knife to Roe.

"A girl can dream." Roe took the knife from her. "Let me live vicariously through you. I just imagine you guys running off, sneaking into hideouts, kissing, and cuddling. He must be warm to cuddle with, right? I mean, they say wolves run hot. I've never encountered one myself, but I think it's true."

"Focus Roe." Kiora laughed. "This is an important mission, not an improper a rendezvous."

"Okay, fine. Just take the fun out of everything." Roe laughed. "Let's get this over with."

Roe cut a lock from her hair the same as Kiora did. Kiora then braided the piece of her hair into the bottom of Roe's braid.

When she was done, Roe did the same, braiding her hair into the bottom of the unraveled braid in Kiora's head.

After the braids were done, they sat across from each other on the ground. Both took a handful of dirt in their right hand. Then they held hands connected their hands in between them. Kiora's left hand over Roe's right and Roe's left hand over Kiora's right. This was the symbol of their connection. They gave silent thanks to the earth for its service as the temporary bond formed between them.

"Can you hear me?" Kiora said thought the question but didn't speak it.

"Yes." Roe responded with her internal voice.

"Good, it worked!" Kiora said aloud. "This should give us a few weeks. Hopefully, that's more than enough time for us to get this done."

"When are you leaving?" Roe stood from the ground and offered Kiora her hand.

"During my next shift." Kiora dusted the dirt from her butt. "I'll need you to cover for me. Can you show up two hours before shift ends?"

"Yea. How are you planning to explain your absence? You know he'll be looking for you." Roe spoke of Marius.

"Let him look. By the time he realizes that I'm not here, I'll be long gone. I'm not here to answer to Marius." Kiora rolled her eyes. "He needs to get over it and move on with his life."

"Okay, you're right." Roe nodded. "And I take it the superiors won't ask questions?"

"That's the best I can come up with now. I'm gonna go get some sleep. I'll see you tomorrow."

Kiora went home, where she slept fitfully. When she woke up, she packed her things, including the clothing Max had delivered to her house. To her relief, Marius was nowhere to be found when she went to the meeting hall.

Same as the day before, she headed out and did her job with heightened awareness. Even though she was leaving, she couldn't slack on her responsibilities before she headed out. The safety of the fairy population still held priority over everything else. Two hours before her shift was supposed to end Roe appeared, yawning, and rubbing her eyes.

"You better be glad I love you." Roe landed the ground next to Kiora. "I should still be asleep right now."

"Your report is in two hours. Why would you still be sleep?" Kiora laughed.

"Hey, not all of us spend our off-time training like you do. I need my beauty rest!" Roe yawned through her joke. "Where's wolf boy?"

"Still in the hideout." Kiora nodded toward the underground space where Raden waited for her.

"I don't even get to see him?" Roe pouted and twirled a braid around her finger.

"Roe." Kiora sucked her teeth. "Can we please be professional?"

"Fine, whatever." Roe waved her off. "Run off and have your fun. I'll just hang out here, watching the trees sway in the wind."

Kiora left her friend who stuck her tongue out at her. She appreciated the humor Roe brought to the situation because she was nervous about what she had to do. Yes, she wanted to help, but if she were honest with herself, the idea of facing vampires terrified her.

"You look a lot better." Kiora commented as she entered the hideout.

Raden sat on the cot opposite the entrance, wrapped in the blanket she left him with.

"I feel better, still not fully healed, but I'm getting there." He waved to her.

"That's good. I brought you some food and clothing. There are also some sanitary items so you can clean up." Kiora tossed the bag to him. "I'll step out while you get dressed."

"You've already seen me naked. Now that I have clothes, you want to walk away?" He laughed. "Interesting."

"I just thought you might want some privacy while you clean up." Kiora explained. "It's not like I had a choice but to see you naked, considering you had no clothing with you."

"Oh, that's right, you fairies aren't used to seeing each other naked." Raden grabbed the bag from the ground where it landed. "It's not that big of a thing for us wolves. How did you know my size?"

"I didn't. But my superior is very intuitive. Besides, I'm sure she has a full profile on you and your entire family." Kiora stayed inside but averted her eyes from his firm ass and thighs. "I've set up everything on my end. So, what's the plan from here?"

58

"You got approval to go with me?" Raden sounded impressed.

"I did and I've arranged for some backup if we shouldn't need it." Kiora said proudly.

"Good." He started his head, looking at the bread. "You smell different. Did you do something?"

"Different?" she frowned.

"Yes." He sniffed at her before he spotted the new color at the end of her braid. "What's that about?"

"It's our insurance policy." She kept her answer short. "Your nose really picked that up?"

"Get enough for me." He shrugged. "And yes, our senses are keen. Even when we aren't in our wolf form. You smell like earth and lavender. That bit in your hair throws it off. Adds a something spicy, like pepper to the scent."

"How do you plan on finding your brother?" Kiora brought the conversation back to their goal and avoided making any comment about how detailed he was in describing her smell.

"We have a link. I can feel him." Raden said as he pulled on the pants. "I know he's still alive, but he's barely holding on. I'll follow the link and it will take me to him."

"Sounds simple. What do you want me to do?" Kiora found herself watching as he used the provided towel and water to clean the dirt from his arms and chest. There was very little bruising left, but she still favored his left side and when he wiped the area he winced.

"Use your fairy powers and protect my brother." Raden continued. "When we get there, you focus on him and him alone. Do whatever you have to do to make sure he gets out safely."

"And what about you?" she asked. "You're not fully healed. Are you going to be able to handle yourself?"

"This isn't about me." Raden pulled the brown shirt from the bag and frowned before pulling it over his head. The material hung from his body like a potato sack. "There is so much more stake."

"The cure." Kiora said.

"You know about that?" He pulled the socks and shoes from the bag.

"Yeah. To be completely transparent, my superior, the one who approved this trip, is sick now." Kiora admitted as Raden finished dressing. "So, I'm hoping that we can save your brother and he can find a cure and save her. She's the closest thing to family I have left."

"Good." He dropped the bag in the corner after pulling the bottle of water out of it.

"Good?" She raised a brow. "It's good that my only family is sick?"

"No, obviously not." He popped the top of the bottle. "But it means you have a real stake in the game now. If you fail, there's more at risk for you."

"Oh." Kiora said. "Strangely insensitive way to look at it."

"I'm sorry. I don't mean to be so analytical. It's just that these things typically work out a lot better when people care about the outcome. You're here to help me and I appreciate that, but at the end of the day there was no real reason for you to stick your neck out for me. Now there is."

"Right. well, eat up. Once you're ready, we can head out. I have a friend in place to cover my position here so we can get a head start before anyone realizes that I'm gone."

"You trying to run outrun someone?" He unwrapped the sandwich she prepared for him.

"That's not important for what we're doing right now." Kiora observed him. "It's just best if we go without witnesses."

"Understood." He bit down into the food and smiled. "As long as it doesn't bring us any problems."

"It won't." The corner of her mouth lifted slightly as she watched him enjoy her food. It was a simple meal, but it had been years since she'd fed anyone other than herself.

"There's something else I need to know about you." Raden spoke around a mouthful of food.

"What's that?" She scratched the back of neck, nervous about what he would want to know.

"Your name. Or should I call you the fairy woman who kidnapped me?" He shoulders shook with the gentle sound of his deep chuckle.

"Kidnapped?!" she scoffed. "Correction. I didn't kidnap you. I saved you."

"I'm joking," he held up his hands to her, a sign of peace he would repeat often. "Chill."

"My name is Kiora." She supplied her name through a tight lip. "You need to work on your comedic delivery. Take a class or something."

"Nice to meet you, Kiora." Raden crossed the space and placed his hand on her shoulder. "Lighten up. I know we're headed off to face down the vampires, but it's okay for you to relax a little."

"Don't tell me to relax." Kiora pointed at him. "Seriously, don't do that."

"Oh, you're right. I forgot. Women hate that. One of those rules that goes across species." He laughed again and grabbed the last bottle of water. "Well, let's get moving."

Six

Twenty minutes later, the wolf and the fairy left Rege. Raden led Kiora away from her home for the first time in nearly ten years. Though she wanted to run off when her sister went missing, Kiora had always been a homebody. She was happy to stay within the confines of their territory, researching their historical data and working on any new findings people like her sister brought home from their excursions.

"Not exactly. It gets stronger as I get closer to him, but I have to use my other senses as well. Where we're headed is about fifteen miles out. We should make it there by nightfall." Raden responded, keeping his careful pace. Though he claimed to be alright, she could tell that he was still hurting.

"Where exactly are we going?" Kiora asked. "I mean, I'm here to help, but it would be nice to know where we're headed."

"I have a friend. He's a wolf, but he's an outsider who lives in the footfalls." Raden sidestepped a squirrel. "If he's still there, he'll give us what we need for the rest of our journey."

"He won't help you?" Kiora smirked at the squirrel, who stopped and eyeballed the man as if he'd tried to kill him. "I mean, he's your friend, can't you recruit him to join us?"

"He's not really the fighter kind, and he stays out of wolf business. A while back, he clarified he didn't agree with the direction our people were going, especially when it came to vampires. He'll give us supplies, maybe some direction, but that's it and that's alright." He looked up at the sky. "I won't ask more of him."

"Understood." Kiora responded. "You respect his boundaries."

"So, tell me more about yourself." Raden looked back at her. "What makes Kiora tick?"

"What do you want to know?"

"Anything you want to share about yourself? We're going to be together for a while. We could travel in silence or spend the time getting to know each other. I'm telling you this walk is going to be mind-numbing if we don't talk."

"Ask me a direct question and I'll answer it." She shrugged. "I don't really like the idea of randomly list off facts about myself. If you leave it up to me, you won't learn anything of value."

"Fair enough." He paused for a moment, considering his first question. "How long have you been a guard?"

"About a year." She answered.

"A newbie and you're already patrolling alone?" He raised a brow. "Interesting."

"Is that not okay?" she asked, annoyed by his insinuation.

"Wouldn't be for wolves, but I guess you guys aren't constantly facing vampire attacks." He said. "It also explains why you would break the rules to help me. Not that I mind. But seasoned guards aren't typically so reckless."

"I don't think I was being reckless." Kiora defended her actions. "But no, we don't deal with the daily threats that you do."

"At least not yet." He grumbled.

"What is that supposed to mean?" She kept her eyes on his back.

"You're smart." He looked her over. "You're not a fighter, at least not yet, but you strike me as the analytical sort. You know how things will go if they take us out. We're their biggest threat. The next on that list, fairies."

"Yeah." She thought about what she said to Max. The vampires would only work their way down the list of threats and take out anyone capable of keeping them in check.

"Why did you become a guard? You don't really seem like the type of person who would want to do this job."

"I lost my sister, and this was the only thing I felt I could do to protect other people from suffering the same way she did." Kiora answered honestly.

"She suffered?" he asked. "How so?"

"I only imagine she did. While she was out on assignment, she unknowingly walked into a vampire feeding ground. They took her and almost every other person on her team."

He stopped and turned to look her in the eye. "I'm sorry that happened."

"Yeah, no one would let me go after her. They said I wasn't stable enough or strong enough." She clinched her jaw.

"That's why you helped me?" Raden connected the dots of her motives.

"Yes." She stopped walking. "When I heard your prayer for your bother, I knew I needed to help you."

"What was your sister doing with her team?" Raden stepped closer to her. "Was it a dangerous mission?"

"It wasn't supposed to be. She was on a convoy. Oddly enough, investigating this disease. It was her job to find out if it would affect our people. She concluded we were safe from it. But it has mutated, as I'm sure you know."

"Yes, it's changed several times, which made it difficult to find a solution for it." He agreed. "My brother was speaking about the rapid mutations when they attacked us. He'd come up with a way to synthesize a medicine that would essentially mutate as needed when it hit the bloodstream and kill the virus, no matter how much it changed."

"That's insanely impressive." Kiora commented. "I'd love to study his notes."

"That isn't the reaction of someone who belongs in the guard." Raden chuckled. "That kid has always been so damn smart. Too smart for his own good sometimes. As you know, he was on his way to finish the cure. It was my job to make sure he got there safely. Not only for the cure, but because of who he is meant to be."

"Who is he meant to be?"

"The next Alpha. Technically, it should be me, but I didn't want that responsibility."

"You can just choose not to be the alpha?" Kiora hadn't read anything about it being a choice in her studies. Her brain shifted into historian mode.

"Yes, of course. It's not forced on us. Besides, it wasn't supposed to be me either." Raden further explained. "I'm the second eldest of four sons, but Rasen died when we were younger, and the responsibility fell to me. I'm not the leader type. I'm more comfortable out in the field. So, it went to Roden. He accepted the honor, and I promised my father that I would protect him from harm and council him when necessary."

"You feel he is better for the job?"

"Hell yeah. The kid is a genius. Our people need someone like him making the tough decisions." He slapped the side of a tree. "I need him to be okay. If not, I'll have to step up and take the role because Rodney is not fit for the role by any means."

"Rodney?"

"Our youngest brother. He's too busy chasing tail to care about the future of our people."

"Your father loved the R names, huh?" Kiora chuckled. "That had to be hard to keep up with."

"Yes, Rasen Sr." He laughed. "Our household was a fun but often confusing place."

Six hours into their trip, they stopped to rest and eat. Kiora watched Raden closely. He still moved like it hurt him to breathe and when he sat down on the tree stump, he winced. Something was wrong. Even with his extensive injuries, the wolf should have been in better condition. He'd had plenty of time to rest. According to her research, even the worst wounds took them about seventy-two hours to heal. After nearly the same time, he was still hurting, but she didn't want to ask about it.

Raden allowed them to rest for thirty minutes, and then they were moving again. As they walked, they shared stories of their childhoods, their families, and their dreams. When Raden asked about Kiora's love life, things got awkward.

"So, there isn't anyone special waiting for you to get back home?" He looked at her through his peripherals.

"No, there isn't." Kiora moved ahead of him to avoid indirect eye contact.

"Why not?" He attempted to continue their conversation.

"Why is that important to what we're doing here?" Kiora responded. Her agitation with the topic was more prevalent.

"It isn't. I thought we were getting to know each other." He held his hands up in defense. "I'd tell you all about my relationship status if you asked."

"I won't." She glanced back at him.

"Right, okay. We're nearly there. I'll go ahead." Raden said when he realized she wouldn't share anymore about the subject.

He pointed to the cabin forty feet ahead of them. "Stay back. He's not a fighter, but he doesn't really take well to unexpected guests."

"Okay." Kiora waved him off. The last thing she wanted was to deal with an agitate wolf. He could smooth things over and then she would approach only when she knew she wouldn't get her head a bit off.

Kiora thought about Raden's question of her relationship status as she watched him approach the home. She didn't mean to snap at him, but the reality was, things were complicated at home. There was no one special in her life because she wasn't interested in anyone. Even if she were, she wouldn't feel comfortable starting something new with her stalker ex-boyfriend all up in her business.

Raden called out his friend's name multiple times but got no response. The closer he got to the house, the more anxious became. He slowed his pace, crouched down, and sniffed the air. Something wasn't right. A moment later, he ran for the door to the cabin, kicked it open and burst inside.

Kiara watched anxiously as he went through the interior of the home. Three long minutes later, Raden exited the house again. He took four steps from the door and then punched the railing at the edge of the porch. The wood snapped with a thunderous sound that echoed in the woods.

"What happened?" Kiora rushed to him.

"He's dead. They got him." Raden screamed. "Those fucking vampires!"

"Are you sure?" She looked at the open door to the house.

"It's a damn bloodbath in there." He pointed to the door. "How the fuck did they even know he was here? The man lived off the damn grid."

"I'm so sorry." Kiora carefully placed a hand on his shoulder.

"Fuck!" He kicked a small bin and sent it flying across the yard and she flinched.

"What can we do? Call someone?" Kiora wanted to do something more than make apologies for something she had no part in.

"There is no one. He was alone." Raden held back tears, but the heaviness of his sorrow cracked his voice.

"Well, he isn't now." She was gentle with her words and replaced her hand on his shoulder. "We're here, Raden."

"Too damn late to help him." His jaw tightened, and he clinched his fist at his side. "What the hell can we do now?"

"Isn't it traditional to bury your dead under the moon?" Kiora tapped into her knowledge of his people. "I've done pretty extensive research of the wolves and I remember how much care you all put into returning your people to the earth. We will honor your friend. Maybe I'm not the adequate companion for this, but I'm here. Whatever you need."

"You would do that?" He turned to face her, and she saw the brim of the tears he held back.

"Yes, because I would want someone to do it for me." Kiora stepped away from him and scanned the area. "Where should we put him to rest? Close to the cabin?"

Raden chose a spot beneath the cover of trees, but one that had a good view of the moon. Kiora used her magic to open the earth, and after careful preparation of the body, which included cleaning the body before they placed it in a gentle wrap made of the leaves from the trees that surrounded his home. The two lowered the man into the earth and Kiora stood by as Raden said his farewell. The only thing Raden couldn't do was the ceremonious howl to the moon.

"Are you sure?" Kiora asked.

"It would be too dangerous. There might be vampires still nearby. I'll shout for him later." Raden put the last of the dirt down. "But thank you for this. For standing with me and saying goodbye to a friend."

He grabbed her hand and held it between his own as he lifted it to his forehead. A show of respect and gratitude.

"You're welcome." Kiora responded and tried to keep the nerves from her voice.

"We need to get going." He looked back at the house. "I don't want to lose too much time. I still feel my brother. It's stronger now. But I don't want to risk it. If they realize I'm nearby, they might move him, or worse."

Luckily, the vampires hadn't found the truck stashed a half mile from the home. They loaded it with food, water, and other supplies that his friend had in a hidden hutch beneath the home. Before the sun rose, and after taking staggering naps, they were on their way.

They drove through the day and as the sun lowered beneath the horizon, Raden felt his connection with his brother strengthen. The wolf's mood shifted, and he gripped the steering wheel as if that would make the vehicle move faster.

"We're close." He said as he cracked the window.

"You're sure?" Kiora straightened in the passenger seat. She'd been slipping into another nap when he spoke.

"Yes, I can feel him and I'm catching his scent now. He is nearby." Raden said as the truck rounded a corner. They were driving through the mountainside. "There are also vampires, though. More of them with each passing minute. The nest must be close by."

"What do we do now?" she asked. "I'm assuming we're not just going to go in and beat down the front door."

"No, we'll find a place to park and scout the area. We need to be smart about this."

Before Raden could map out anymore of his plan, something hit the side of the truck, causing it to swerve on the curved road. Kiora looked out the window just in time to see the first vampire move away and the second one slam into them, which sent the massive vehicle spinning. They crashed into a guardrail and then the truck flipped.

Kiora barely put together what was happening before Raden was out of the truck and fighting. Sounds of growls, screams, and crunching metal filled her ears as she tumbled with the truck. She landed on her back on the roof of the overturned vehicle.

As she watched someone walk towards her through the shattered window, she struggled to hold on to her consciousness. She had no idea who it was, but she knew they weren't there to help her. Her stomach flooded with a rush of chaotic energy that told her she had to get out of there, but the seatbelt had wrapped around her leg, trapping her in place.

Kiora let her instincts guide her. She reached out the window and placed her hand on the dirt. In a simultaneous effort, the earth came to her aid. The ground beneath the vampire who approached her shot up around it and trapped in the temporary hold while the dirt beneath the truck lifted to flip the vehicle upright again so Kiora could get out.

As she stumbled out of the door, she faced the vampire, who continuously punched their way out of the dirt jail. Each time they made a break in the trap, new earth lifted to replace it. Kiora took her opportunity quickly. She grabbed a stake out of the back seat and went for the vampire and drove the weapon through their heart just as the dirt opened to give her clear access to their chest. The vampire screamed out, then burst into flames, quickly turning to ash.

"Thank you." Kiora said to the earth before running to find Raden.

By the time she made it to him, he'd already taken out the two vampires he'd battled with.

"Are you okay?" he looked at her, his body returning from his wolf form.

"I'm good, are you?" She worried about his injuries. Shifting had to have caused more damage.

"Yes," he said, then stumbled. "We need to get out of here. More are coming. We won't survive."

"They wrecked the truck." She pointed to their ride. "It's not moving again."

"Forget it. Take what we can and run." He limped over to the truck and forced the back door to open so they could grab supplies including new clothes for him.

"You don't look like you can run." She started grabbing things from the truck and handed a bag to him.

"I'll live." He muttered, holding his side as he moved.

They took only what they could carry without slowing them down, then headed down the side of the mountain to avoid the road. Which would make them easy targets. Their descent was more sliding than controlled movements and when they reached the second plateau, Kiora called an end to it.

"Okay, that's enough. You need to rest."

"We stop here and we're sitting ducks." He refused. "It won't take them long to find us here."

"No, we aren't" She placed her hand against the side of the mountain, and it opened for her. What was once a solid wall became the opening to a cavern big enough for two. "Get in." She instructed him.

They stepped inside, and she placed her hand against the interior wall, and asked the earth to move for her again. And it did. The entrance closed, leaving only three small tunnels for air to get in.

"Thank you," she said to the earth.

"That's a neat trick." Raden said before coughing and spitting up blood.

"I told you; you're too injured for this." She rushed to his side.

"I'm fine, I'll heal." He repeated what was feeling like a lie to her.

"You keep saying that, but are you really okay? I'm looking at you and I'm not seeing much healing happening now."

"I'm okay," Raden said again, but then he dropped. Like a brick in a pool. His back slammed against the ground. "Okay, you might be right." He choked.

"Do you trust me?" She knelt beside him.

"Why do you ask?" he looked up at her. "That's what my brother would ask me before he followed it up with some crazy plan that he knew I wouldn't like."

"I think I know something that can help, but I'm basically going to have to bury you to do it."

"Bury me?" He coughed again. "Yeah, no, I'm not about to do that."

He clutched the side of the dirt wall in attempt to regain his footing but fell, this time hitting his back on the wall.

"Do you want to save your brother or now?"

"Yes," he looked at her. "Of course, I do."

"Well, shouldn't you be at your best? You go into a fight with the vampires like this, and you both die. And possibly me too."

She touched his shoulder. "I like you and all, but I'm not trying to die here."

"Fuck." He thought about what she said. "Fine. Do it."

Moments later, Raden climbed into the ground, and she buried completely his body beneath the dirt, only his face visible. This was a healing treatment and a closed practice usually done in the forest around their home, but it was the only thing she could think of. When the earth sealed around him and the magic stated working, he passed out.

Kiora lay beside him, hand on the side of his face, and prayed for healing. She asked the earth, the oceans, and the moon above to heal his body, heart, and mind so they he could save his brother.

Seven

While Raden slept, Kiora watched him. She tracked his breathing and when the sweat formed on his brow, she ripped the bottom of her shirt, wet it, and dabbed his forehead. There was no way to tell how he would respond to the treatment. The best thing she could do was keep him comfortable.

For a while, Raden muttered in his sleep between shallow breaths. And then he stopped. All semblance of activity ceased, and he looked like a statue sticking out of the ground.

"Please don't die." Kiora whispered to him, not that he could hear her with his ears covered.

She placed her palm on the dirt that covered his body and asked the earth to tell her how he was. The response was positive. Through the pulses returned to her, she felt his life strengthening. The magic worked to heal his body, but something was wrong. Something deeper than his physical injuries. She wished she knew what it was, and how to help him.

The pulses also told her something else. Something more alarming. The vampires, the ones who wanted to kill them were getting closer. She closed her eyes and let her connection to the earth take over her. Kiora's mind became an extension of the soil, and she could feel everything the surrounding land did. She felt the animals that lived in the vicinity, the plants connected to it, the roots in the ground, and Raden.

She barely caught the activity, but it was there. Light, calculated, and deadly. Footfalls of hunters searching for their prey. Kiora could feel their intention, their murderous desires. They were out for blood.

She opened her eyes to look down at Raden's face and then glance at the air tunnels. If they got close enough, they could smell his blood. It wasn't a lot, but it was enough. She couldn't risk them being found. Neither would survive if the vampires tore down the barrier that kept them hidden.

Soon she would have to close the tunnels. She kept her hand to the ground to monitor their progress. Though she wished they would change their path, they continued moving directly for them. She would hold out as long as she could.

"Fuck," she muttered, then pulled the braid blended with Roe's hair from the bun at the back of her neck. "I didn't want to have to do this so soon."

Kiora placed the end of the braid to her lips and whispered her friend's name. "Roe, hear me, answer my call." She then touched the braid to her forehead and a moment later, her eyes lit up.

Her mind emptied and all sense of the world around her faded as she entered the metaphysical space where she awaited the woman she called out to.

"Kiora?" Roe answered her, her voice groggy with interrupted sleep.

"Roe." Kiora stood in the airy space wrapped in gray wisps of fabric.

"You in trouble already?" Kiora appeared, wearing the same tendril-like attire.

"Unfortunately." Kiora answered. "And I don't have much time."

"What do you need?" Roe sobered up.

"We're close to his brother, but we're trapped." Kiora reported their situation. "They attacked us and had to take cover underground. But the vampires haven't given up and they are getting closer to our location. I'm using the earth to monitor their position, but soon I'm going to have to close off our air. Raden is bleeding, so if they get too close, they'll be able to sniff us out. I need you and the others to come save us."

"Damn it. That's not good." Roe bit her lip. "Are you injured?"

"I'm okay. A little beat up, but nothing major. I'll survive. I'm trying to use a submersion to heal him, though I don't know how his body will react to it." Kiora checked out of the mental connection for a moment to monitor the vampires. There wasn't much time. She checked by in. "Can you find us?"

"Yea, give me your hand." Roe held her hand out to Kiora, who grasped it.

Their hands blended and became an expanding ball of light that tapped into both energetic beings to create a deeper connection between the two. Flashes of Kiora's travels moved from her mind to become implanted in Roe's memory. It would be as if Roe walked the path herself.

"Got it." Roe let her go. "We're coming. How long do you have?"

"I don't know. They're close, so I'll have to seal us off." Kiora looked back over her shoulder as if she could feel the vampires on top of her. "Just hurry, please."

"We're on our way. Hold tight." Roe nodded to her friend and then ended the conversation.

With the connection ended, Kiora turned her attention back to the vampires. They were minutes away, which meant she was out of time. Soon they'd pick up his scent. Reluctantly, she asked the earth to do the only thing she could think of to save their lives.

"Please, seal the airways." She said in a soft and fearful voice.

She lay on the ground next to Raden and placed her hand on his face as the airways closed.

"We're going to be okay." she whispered to him and then she slowed her breathing. It was a technique taught to her by her mother. The strengthening of her lungs meant should survive with less air. It would also mean more for Raden.

She closed her eyes, allowing the conservation of air to calm her body. If she didn't, she would go into shock. It would be only a few more moments before she drifted to sleep but her breathing would remain the same.

She only hoped Roe would make it to them in case she didn't wake again.

BREAK

Kiora spent the next three hours fading in and out of consciousness. When she could, she checked the area for the vampires, but they were unrelenting in their search. Just as the burn set in her chest, an indicator that they were almost out of air, she felt them retreating from the area. But it wasn't a quiet evacuation. Something riled up the vampires before they left.

It didn't matter. She thanked the goddess for whatever called the threat away and when she felt they were safe; she asked the earth to open just one airway. It wouldn't be much, but it would keep them from dying and make it easier for Roe and the others to find them. Still lightheaded and keeping her breathing monitored, she passed out again.

"Kiora." The muffled voice nudged Kiora from her sleep. Her keen ears vibrated as she tried to focus on the sound. She nearly went back to sleep, but the voice called her again. "Kiora, are you in there?"

"Roe?" Kiora whispered the name of her friend. "Is that you?"

"Open up and let us in, please. None of us can talk to the earth like you can." Roe answered her. "We're here to help."

"You're here?" Kiora's mind struggled to process what was happening.

"Yes, and we need to get in there before your blood suckers circle back around." Roe's comment snapped Kiora into focus.

"Shit." she placed her palm on the earth and asked it to clear the way for her friend.

It responded, clearing the path, and allowing a gush of fresh air to enter the cave with the moonlight. There, silhouetted in the moon, was Roe.

"You made it." Kiora filled her lungs with air. "Thank you."

"Hey, I said I would be here." Roe looked around the small space. "You think you can give us a bit more room? I doubt we're all going to fit in here. Barely enough room for the two of you."

"Oh, the others. Where are they?" Kiora looked around her friend to the empty entrance.

"They're scouting the area. We created a diversion to drive the vampires away. I have them getting a lay of the land and just making sure we're in the clear."

"Roe," Kiora stood from her place on the ground and hugged Roe. "I'm so happy to see you."

"Of course, you are, I'm pretty amazing." Roe laughed. "So, give us more room?"

"Right." Kiora placed her hand on the curved wall of dirt and stone and asked the earth to move yet again. What was a space big enough for two slowly eased into one that could fit ten. "Good enough?"

"Yes, perfect." Roe dropped her eyes to the face that stuck out from the dirt. "I take it that's Raden?"

"Yes, it is." Kiora confirmed.

"All clear." Sky said as she landed at the entrance. Her blue uniform and wings blended almost seamlessly with the wash of moonlight. She brushed the short blue dyed hair from her face. She'd cut it into a pixie cut because she said it was easier to deal with in the shorter state.

"Same. The vampires aren't coming back this way. The sun will be up soon." Marley a man with reddish brown skin and wings that matched reported as he landed behind Sky. He threw his arm around her shoulder and kissed her forehead. "Miss me babe?"

"Always." Sky winked at him and threw her arm around his waist.

"Great. Still, to be sure, I think I'll close up the doorway." Roe placed her hand on the curved wall, prepared to ask the earth to move again.

"Wait," Roe put her hand on Kiora's arm. "There's one more."

"What?" Kiora frowned. "I only asked you to talk to two people, Roe. Do you know how much danger you could have put them in? Who is it?"

"Kiora." The voice was like a cheese grater on her brain. It made her skin crawl and her stomach knot up. Marius.

"What the hell is he doing here?" Kiora asked Roe who was responsible for getting their team together. "Of all the people you could have brought with you. Why him?"

"You know damn well I didn't invite him." Roe pointed to the man who stood behind Kiora. "The jerk caught us leaving and insisted on tagging along."

"Just talk about me like I'm not standing right here." Marius spoke up. "That's not very nice."

"Shut up." Kiora snapped at him without turning to face him.

"Kiora, I just wanted to make sure you were alright." he has the explanation no one asked him for.

"I'm fine." She turned to him and waved her hands up the length of her body. "Now that you see that, you can go home."

"Are you seriously denying my offer of help when your life is in danger?" he called out her shortsightedness. "I know you may hate me right now, but do you really care so little about your own safety?"

Kiora thought about it. As much as she wanted him to be wrong, he wasn't. Stalker or not, Marius was a powerful fairy, and he had more field experience than all of them combined. He could prove useful for their mission.

"No, I guess I'm not." She responded.

"What's up with him?" Sky pointed to the face of the man beneath the ground. "I mean not to interrupt this interesting conversation, but is this the guy we're out here trying to help?"

"Yes, it is." Kiora stepped closer to Raden with a sudden urge to protect him. "The vampires attacked us. We won, but not without injury. He's healing. Should be able to come out of it soon."

"We're just sitting here until then?" Marius asked. "Is that really what you're planning to do now?"

"What else would we do?" Kiora turned on him. "You have any other brilliant ideas?"

"Leave him here." he said coldly.

"Are you insane?" she snapped. "You would leave him here to die?"

"Why risk your life for him?" Marius shrugged. "He's a wolf. He can handle himself. You can ask the earth to release him when he's healthy enough, can't you?"

"You really are an asshole, you know that?" Roe leaned against the wall of the cavern. "I mean, we all joke about it, but you prove it more and more every time you open your mouth."

"Kiora." Marius ignored Roe's comment. "Listen to me, please. You need to do what is safest for yourself."

"Stop saying my name like that." Kiora hated the way he softened his voice when he spoke her name like he did when they were together. It hinted at a level of affection that no longer fit their relationship. "Besides, when I signed up to be a guard, it was to protect other people."

"Our people." Marius repeated her words to her. "Exactly. Wolves are not our people."

"Helping him will help to protect our people. I'm not turning my back on him like some coward." She jabbed. "I know that's what you prefer I do. Just like with Safir."

"It makes no sense to keep doing this. You've already failed. They know you're here and they know who he is. They will only increase whatever protections they have around his brother." Marius pointed out every flaw he could find in her plans.

"I don't need your opinions or permission. You chose to come here, and you can very well choose to fly your ass back home, but I'm not leaving without him." Kiora held her ground. "I made a promise to him. And unlike some people, when I make a promise, I keep my word. It matters to me."

"Whatever." he threw his hands up. "We wait."

Kiora placed her hand on the wall and asked the earth to close the entrance behind Marius and kept enough airways to allow for the six people inside to breathe. It closed, and they all sat down along the wall, Kiora closest to Raden.

"I guess we can rest now, right? I could use a nap after that flight." Marley yawned and stretched as he leaned against the dirt wall.

"Yeah, rest up. I'll keep watch." Kiora said. "I've slept plenty."

While the others settled in to sleep, Kiora watched Raden. His breathing was better. She touched the earth, asking for an update, and found relief when the response was positive. He would wake soon. Which was good because she didn't trust Marius. Everything about him being there felt wrong, and not just because he was a stalker who wouldn't leave her alone.

Eight

An hour later, the others had all drifted to sleep while Kiora kept watch. From time to time, she placed her palm against the ground to check for t vampires. Though with the sun rising soon, they wouldn't have to worry about the blood suckers finding them for much longer. Kiora was content to sit with her thoughts. There was a lot she had to consider, like the wolf buried in the ground and the fairy who wanted to leave him behind. She needed a plan, preferably one that would send Marius away from them.

She calculated her options, before a familiar tingling in her mind took her away from the hideout and into the metaphysical space that she shared with her friend Roe.

"Why are we here?" Kiora walked over to Roe in the hazy space. "You're right next to me. You know you can just tell me what you want."

"Obviously we're here because there is something I have to tell you that the others cannot know." Roe jutted her neck at Kiora. "Think girl."

"Necessary secrecy. That can't be good." Kiora rubbed the sides of her forehead. "What is it?"

"Marius is not to be trusted." Roe issued her warning. "I don't think he is really on our side."

"No shit." Kiora roller her eyes. "The man is obsessed, and it's blinding him."

"There's more to it than that." Roe shook her head. "Max sent a message to me. It said she doesn't trust him. Apparently, the superiors have suspected him for a while now. Meaning, he's made them think he isn't as trustworthy as he wants everyone to believe."

"Seriously?" Kiora gawked. "What do they think he's done?"

"Max didn't tell me all the details, but it sounds like the others weren't so blinded to his actions all this time like we thought they were. It started before your sister died, but Max picked up on the way he reacted to you when everything happened."

"What do you mean?"

"Well, she spoke about a few things that they found alarming. Like how he got upset anytime you talked about leaving the city. It wasn't just about your sister. He wasn't afraid of the vampires hurting you because you were out for vengeance. He doesn't want you outside of Rege at all. And the way he's been relentlessly stalking you since it happened just proves that there is something more going on with him." Roe repeated the information given to her.

"Also, Max said on a few of his trips, he showed some concerning behavior patterns. Disappearing when he should have been reporting in, ignoring all kinds of protocols, making excuses to extend his time in the field, and refusing to share details about his new informants with the others. Whatever is going on with Marius, it's bad and Max told me to make sure you watch her back with him."

"I can't believe this. I mean, I knew something was wrong with having him here. And lately, any time I'm around him, I feel like my skin is going to crawl right off of me. But I thought it was because of my own personal issues with him and you're telling me now that there's something more dangerous happening?"

"I wish I could give you a better answer, Kiora. All I know is that Max wants you to proceed with extreme caution with him here. She doesn't trust him and apparently a lot of the others don't either. Outside of that, I don't really know what else to say."

"Thank you for telling me." Kiora took a deep breath. "What the hell are we supposed to do now? I wanted to get away from Marius but now that I know the superiors don't trust him either, I'm not sure if it's best to send him away."

"Do you really think you can find his brother?" Roe asked. "Raden's hurt, and he's also the only one with a connection to his brother. How are we going to get to him?"

"Raden is healing. He will be okay, and I already know he can find him. We aren't that far away. That's why the vampires attacked us." Kiora explained. "Either way, I'm not about to turn my back on him, especially when there's so much riding on this."

"I understand." Roe watched Kiora. The subtle tapping of her foot and nibbling on her lip mean there was more she wanted to say but hadn't found the words or courage to do so.

"Do you still have my back on this?" Kiora asked. "This is getting a lot more complicated than we planned."

"Always girl, you know that." Roe winked. "Complicated is my love language. You know that."

"We should get back to reality. I really don't trust Marius enough to leave him out there with Raden." Kiora couldn't feel what went on in the real world while in their mental connection. Even with her hand still on the ground.

"You're right. He probably knows you're tapped out." Roe nodded and stepped back from Kiora, fading away.

"Stop!" Roe's yelled order registered to Kiora before she fully returned to consciousness.

Kiora opened her eyes to see Marius standing over her with murderous intent in his expression. She jumped to her feet, putting herself between him and the man buried beneath the ground.

"What the hell do you think you're doing?" She held her hands up, ready to fight him If necessary. "Back the hell up."

"I'm just checking on our patient." Marius looked at her, then glanced at Raden's face.

"Yeah right. You need to step back, right now." Kiora warned him. "I'm serious Marius, don't make me hurt you."

"Listen, I get you don't like me." he leaned in close to her, lowering his voice. "But do not disrespect me, Kiora. I am your superior even if you don't want me in your life. You joined the guard, and you will stay in your place."

"You are an unwelcome guest on *my* mission." Kiora corrected him. "No matter your rank on the guard, I'm in control here. I don't have to show you any more respect than you show me, and I don't give a damn about whatever title you think you hold over me. If you don't like it, you can go home."

"That's it. I'm sick of this. We are leaving." Marius wrapped his hand around Kiora's wrist and pulled her with him. "We're going home."

"Let me go!" Kiora smacked the wall, and the earth responded, shooting stone at Marius' face and shoulder. When he shielded his face, he let Kiora go, and she fell against the wall.

"Son of a bitch!" Marius yelled and lunged for her.

Just then Raden's eyes opened, and he spoke her name. She touched the ground and told the earth to free him and a moment later, he burst out of the dirt. Raden tackled the fairy who approached her. His fist slammed into Marius's chest, knocking him against the outer wall which crumbled around him before it quickly repaired itself.

"Keep your hands off her!" Raden yelled.

Marius straightened quickly and pulled a blade from his side, ready to fight the wolf.

"You think you can take me, bring it on!" Marius yelled out.

Raden growled, ready to shift and rip the man apart.

"Raden, it's okay." Kiora stepped in between them and looked Raden in the eye. "Don't do this. He isn't worth it."

"Don't want to mess up your chances of saving your brother, now do we?" Marius taunted him. "Better check your temper, wolf."

"Raden." Kiora said his name, pulling his attention back to her. "Let it go. Please."

"Fine." Raden sniffed the air and narrowed his eyes at Marius. "Watch your back."

"Good boy." Marius teased and Raden responded with a warning growl.

"Chill!" Kiora yelled.

"I'm cool." Marius held his hands up.

"Might want to carve out a bigger space in here." Sky muttered.

"We won't be here much longer, anyway." Kiora said. "We need to make a move. The vampires know we're here and they will come back to find us."

"Maybe they'll think we used the daylight to leave." Sky offered.

"No." Raden spoke. "They know I won't leave without my brother."

"Great, you're determined to get your brother." Marley sighed, arm still around Sky. "Where does that leave us? There is still the matter of the murderous vampires who stand between us and him."

"We've definitely lost the element of surprise here." Roe agreed and leaned against the wall next to Marley. "So, we can't rely on that anymore. What we need is to get inside and eliminate the risk of them cutting our heads off at the damn door."

"So, what you're saying is that we're headed into a battle that we may not make it out of? Great! That's exactly why I signed up for this job." Sky scoffed. "I definitely don't get paid enough for this."

"We can't think like that." Kiora debated their outlook. "For all we know, we'll get in and out with no problem."

"It must be nice to have such optimism on your side." Marley laughed. "Just in and out of a vampire's nest without a scratch."

"Hey, I'm just choosing to not assume we're all going to die here." Kiora responded. "Thinking like that is only going to make our jobs harder and make it so we end up dead. And I don't know about you, but I want to make it home."

"You're right." Raden agreed with Kiora. "It's good to recognize the facts, but we have to go into this confident and careful of our actions. The vampires are smart, and they've been working on this plan for a long time. They snatched my brother because they know about his potential. They know what he's capable of, and they aren't going to just sit back and let us take him home."

"All this mental courage is nice and well, but do any of you have an actual plan?" Marius laughed dryly. "Sure, we go in confident. What the hell are we doing when we get there?"

"You're assuming you're still invited?" Kiora frowned at him.

"I'm not letting you go in there without me." Marius asserted. "It's dangerous in there and you're going to need me."

"You already tried to attack her." Roe reminded him of the threat he presented. "You're out of your mind."

"We can use him." Raden said. "Besides, he's going to act accordingly. I'm not the only one with something on the line."

"What do you mean by that?" Kiora asked, her suspicions about Marius peaking again.

"He means you." Marius blurted out before Raden could speak. "I don't want to lose you, Kiora."

"Yeah," Raden nodded. "That's exactly what I mean."

"Okay..." Roe interrupted the awkward moment. "Someone was going to lie out a plan for us?"

"Vampire compounds are all the same." Raden started. "They've been around for centuries and they're creatures of habit. From my estimation, we're about five miles outside of their outer boundary. That means we're five miles away from their familiars. Mostly humans who have agreed to work with them in exchange for protection. They're the ones who watch over the vampire territories during the day when they cannot do it themselves." Raden used the end of a stake to draw a diagram in the dirt.

"That barrier wall is typically about a mile and a half to two miles from the main wall. The main wall is where they'll have their secondary line of defense, which is typically protected by magic workers. Humans during the day, vampires at night."

"Witches too?" Roe asked. "Is that a possibility?"

"Yes, and considering my brother is here, it would stand to chance they have someone strong. Someone capable of really doing some serious damage. Once we get past that line, we will be inside the hearts of vampire territory."

"Then what?" Marley asked. "We get by the humans and the witches and then?"

"I'm assuming they have my brother in the heart of their territory, which means going through at least three more sections that will be full of vampires. Even if we move during the day, we won't have the advantage. We'll be underground. There will be no sunlight to work on our side.

"If that's the case, shouldn't we have more people on our side with this? I mean, you're talking about running into a fucking fortress and I'm sorry, but I don't think the six of us are enough." Marley stood from his seat on the floor.

"Actually, our small numbers will benefit us. Right now, the vampires only think that there are two of us, which means we have four people who can work as an element of surprise." Raden glanced at Marius, and Kiora followed the quick look. Raden didn't trust Marius, and he wasn't the only one.

"They also don't know about your abilities." Raden continued. "Everyone knows that fairies have powers, but we don't know what power you possess because it changes from fairy to fairy. Kiora clearly has a connection to Earth. What about the rest of you?"

"Air." Sky raised her hand.

"Fire is my thing." Marley tilted his head and flared his fingers, though he brought no flame to his hand.

"I have a combination of air and water." Roe offered and after a long pause, all eyes turned to Marius, who chose not to reveal his power.

"Marius is also air." Kiora told spoke for him.

"Perfect. From the sounds of it, we have some pretty powerful people on our side, which means we can come up with a solid strategy for both defense and offense." Raden continued. "We will go underground. They won't be expecting us to move beneath them. Which means we can completely bypass the first two barriers outside of their territory. Keep in mind that if they have someone powerful enough at the second line, they may detect us, so we'll have to be careful."

"We can cushion any sound we make with air." Roe offered. "We'll have to move a little slower, but it's worth it if we don't have to encounter witches."

"Sounds good to me." Raden nodded. "Once we're there, we'll use a combination of the other's skills to fight. We'll have to be precise with every movement we make once we're inside.

"When we get my brother, Kiora, you will break open an alternative path. The entire structure is all made of the earth, so it should be no problem for you to create a path. And then we'll fly the hell right out of there."

"You make it sound so easy." Marius spoke, clearly unimpressed with the plan Raden laid out.

"It won't be easy. But this is the best shot that we have. I don't know what you plan to do, but I will not miss my shot. I'm getting my brother the hell out of there."

"When do we leave?" Sky impressed with Raden's determination.

"Now." Raden said. "While the sun is still up. We can make most of our progress while they are down for the day. If they wake and move around the mountainside, it's going to make us a lot more vulnerable than we already are."

"Great, lead the way, wolf man." Marius mocked him.

Raden walked over to Marius, and everyone in the hideout froze. He leaned close to the man and spoke so only he could hear the threat.

"When this is over, I'm going to rip your head from your shoulders."

Nine

T he team worked together effortlessly. Kiora chose Roe and the others because of their history. When she first became a guard, Marley, Sky, and Roe were there to help her train. And the three of them developed an almost psychic connection that made it easier for them to blend their forces.

To begin, Kiora laid one hand on the earth and the other on Raden's shoulder. She cleared her mind and spoke to the earth. "Use his connection with his brother to guide us. Open safe passage so that we may bring him home."

A moment later, the left wall shifted and a tunnel just wide enough for them to move in pairs opened.

"Not a lot of space." Sky poked her head into the tunnel. "I'm not a big girl, but I would like to stretch out a little."

"We don't want it to be that much space." Kiora responded. "This way, we don't have to disrupt the soil above us. And what we move will simply be displaced behind us."

"Does that mean we can get trapped in there? What if we run out of air?" Marley raised his hand. "Forget about stretching. I'm opposed to suffocation."

"We won't. There will be enough flowing for them to muffle our movement, and for us to breathe. We are safe." Kiora reassured him.

"Good." Raden nodded. "Let's get going."

Roe and Sky took the lead, and as the earth shifted to clear their path, they cycled the air to muffle the sound. Raden and Kiora remained in the middle. Kiora kept her hand on Raden's shoulder and the other to the side of the wall, reinforcing the connection between the earth and the wolf. In the back, Marley monitored Marius, who also used the air to cushion the sounds of their footfalls.

"How much further do you think we have to go?" Marley asked after they'd been moving for an hour.

"Not far, maybe another mile or two." Raden answered. "I can feel him a lot stronger. We're close."

"Meaning we've already passed the outer borders?" Marley asked.

"I would say yes, we have." Raden nodded.

"And not one witch sensed us?" Roe glanced over her shoulder at them. "I mean, I know we're good at what we do, but what are the odds that this would go over so smoothly?"

"Let's not question our good fortune here." Marley called out. "At least not until we're out of this place."

"Fine, but I'm telling you, something is up with this." Roe responded, brushing away dirt that fell in her hair. "I was expecting at least a little push back."

Raden looked at Kiora, a frown on his face.

"Are you worried?" Kiora asked him.

"No, but she's right. Something's up. I can feel it." Raden answered. "I've been in this position plenty of times, and this isn't how it usually works. Granted, we're not typically underground when it happens."

"Okay, so what are you thinking?" Kiora nudged him. "What do you want to do?"

"I'll keep my thoughts to myself for now, if you don't mind." He answered. "We're on the path. We stay the course."

"Alright." Kiora accepted his decision without further question.

They continued, still uninhibited by any outside force. By the time they came to a stop, Roe wasn't the only one suspicious of their effortless approach.

"There is a room on the other side of this wall." Kiora told them when they stopped. "Once we break through, we'll be out in the open."

"Can you tell what it is?" Roe asked. "What are we up against?"

"Yeah, give me a second." Kiora touched the wall, and the earth gave her a vision of the space on the opposite side. "It's a full underground compound. Just like Raden said. They carved all the rooms into the ground. Few artificial support structures to help. It looks like there are four rooms between us and Raden's brother. We can cut right through easily, but-"

"But what?" Roe asked when Kiora hesitated. "What is it?"

"No one's there." Kiora frowned. "I don't sense any people."

"What do you mean?" Raden moved closer to her.

"Usually I can feel movement." Kiora explained. "Anything that contacts the earth that I'm surveying. There is only one person in the center of what I think is a pit, four rooms over. And that's it."

"So, we're in a vampire nest and there are no vampires, even though it's the middle of the day?" Roe scoffed. "Again, I say, something is up with this shit."

"That's what it feels like." Kiora confirmed. "If they are here, they have a hell of a way of hiding their presence."

"What are the odds that this isn't a total trap?" Marley asked from the back of the group.

"I'm going to say that it's pretty damn impossible for this not to be a trap right now." Sky leaned against the wall.

"So, we're on the same page." Marley clapped. "Good to know."

"The sun is going to set soon. So even if they're all just sleeping, they'll wake up and realize we're here." Roe pointed out their timing. "We need to figure out what to do next."

"It's all too damn easy. Not one alert. They already know we're here." Marius paced the tiny space and rubbed the back of his neck with his hands.

"What do we do?" Roe asked.

"We continue." Raden spoke for the first time. "We're already here. Turning back is not an option."

"They have to know we're here." Marley huffed. "We're just accepting that fact? If they know, that means they're prepared for us."

"If they do, why would they let us get this far inside?" Kiora asked. "Why risk letting us get to him?"

"Because they don't think we'll be able to get him out of here." Roe shrugged. "They know if we're sneaking in, our numbers aren't large enough to make any real noise. Vampires are sick creatures. This is all a game for them. And we just played right into it."

"Fuck." Sky said. "I knew we should have gotten more back up for this."

"We didn't have time for that. Besides, there's nothing saying that bringing more people into this would have been the smart thing to do." Kiora said.

"It's a damn trap." Marius said. "We've figured that out. Wolf man here wants to keep going. I don't, but it's not my mission, right?"

He looked at Kiora, and all eyes went to her.

"So, what do you say, oh leader? You want to keep going and risk getting us all killed in there? This is what you wanted, right?

To take charge, well, the decision is yours to make." Marius tried to shake her resolve.

Kiora looked around at the group of people who watched and waited for her decision. Roe was down with whatever she chose. Marley looked annoyed. Sky looked nervous. Marius clearly wanted her to retreat but Raden. Raden looked as though it didn't matter to him what her decision was. He was moving ahead with or without the others.

On top of the heavy weight of their expectation was the rising heat in the tunnel and the stench from the blood-soaked earth nearby. This was a vampire nest, she reminded herself, that the blood was to be expected. Again, she looked at Raden and her decision was clear. She'd made a promise to him. She told him she would help him find his brother, and she intended to keep that promise.

"We're going ahead." Kiora looked Marius in the eye. "If you're so afraid, turn tail and run, though I'm not sure the earth will remain open for you once I'm away, so you'll have to take your chances above ground."

"This is a mistake." Marius insisted. "We should turn back."

"The only mistake was you allowing you to be here." Kiora responded. "But you insisted on coming. So, deal with it."

"It's not the right choice. It's a trap. Why are you being so damn stubborn about this?" Marius narrowed his gaze on Kiora and the hurt flashed in his eyes. "For this wolf? Are you seriously so blinded by your lust?"

"Lust?" Kiora scoffed. "So, according to you, the only reason I would do the right thing is if I'm driven by lust?"

"Kiora, I'm not a fucking idiot." he pointed at her. "You're doing this, and it's not just because you care about someone you've never met before."

"Back off." Kiora pointed back at him. "I'm sick of this."

"I'm serious." Marius continued. "You-,"

"We don't have time for this shit." Raden interrupted their debate. "Whatever is going on between you two, work it out when we're not standing outside a vampire's nest. Trap or not, I'm getting to my brother. Kiora, open the way."

Without another word, Kiora pressed her hand against the dirt wall and the earth moved out of the way, opening up to the large room on the other side. It was more than they expected it to be. It was like stepping into a museum. Fully refined but crafted from the earth showing much more respect than Kiora thought possible of the vampires. Lanterns lined the walls, every other one lit and cast a soft glow in the space.

"Woah," Sky huffed as she stepped through. "This is insane. Look at this place."

"If it wasn't a den for monsters, I'd find this impressive." Marley put his hand on her shoulder, then reached up to the lantern next to him and grabbed the flame. He rolled it across his fingers and sighed. "Finally, I can work my magic."

"Let's move." Raden looked at Kiora. "What's the best path?"

Kiora pointed to the door across from them. "Through there is a line of connected doorways. Almost a straight path."

"Good." Raden took the lead, walking towards the door.

"Yep, straight into the trap." Marley followed behind him, rolling the flames on both hands.

The group moved ahead, passing through empty rooms lined with the same lanterns. Raiden and Marley took the lead while Roe covered the rear. The first two rooms were simple, straight shots with nothing to worry about, but before they could make it through the third, a blast shook the walls. The six intruders braced, expecting an onslaught. They watched the doorways, but nothing came.

"What the hell was that?" Marius asked.

"An explosion, obviously." Sky responded, holding her position, air at the ready.

Kiora knelt and touched the ground. "Shit."

"What is it?" Raiden asked her. "What's wrong?"

"The last doorway. It's closed." She looked up at him. "They cut us off from Roden."

"Dammit." Raiden took off running, and the others followed him. Just as Kiora said, on the opposite side of the fourth room was a collapsed doorway.

"He's on the other side. I can feel it." Kiora called out. "I can move the earth. We just need to be ready when that wall comes down. Clearly, we aren't alone."

"Do you feel anyone else over there?" Roe asked.

"No, just one person. Feels like he's sitting in a chair." Kiora reported.

"Okay, let's get him." Raiden said. "Take it down."

Kiora looked at the others and waved them back. When they were at a safe distance, she placed her hand on the wall and a moment later, the fallen earth parted. And on the other side, there was darkness. The room was twice the size of the others and had very little light given off by only two lanterns in the far corners of the room, though there were others.

"Trap for sure. Why is it so dark in here?" Sky stepped through the opening.

"Marley, get us some more light in here?" Kiora asked.

"My pleasure." Marley shot a flame from his fingertip, and it bounced from lantern to lantern, lighting up the circular room.

This one was different. There were no sophisticated finishing touches, no smooth flooring. Just a round platform carved into the dirt with a pit in the center of the room.

"He's in there." Kiora pointed to the hole ahead of them. "I can feel him."

"Yea, I can too." Raden ran forward despite the threat of attack and the other followed him.

Kiora touched the wall, calling the earth to her hand, and it attached to her like a glove. As she walked, a pillar of earth moved with her like an extension to the earth that would work to protect her. Each person kept their eyes on the perimeter, all but Marius who lingered behind the others and stayed close to the door.

"Dammit," Raden stood at the edge of the pit looking down on his brother, who they'd tied to a chair. "I can smell the blood."

"Is that him?" Kiora looked over her shoulder at him. "Are you sure?"

"Yes." Raden confirmed before he jumped into the pit.

"Roden." Raden grabbed his brother's face between his hands. He wiped the blood from his brow. "You're alive."

"Raden, no." his brought coughed dryly, and looked at Raden through swollen eyes. "Why did you come?"

"You know damn well why I came." Raden worked to remove the ropes around his brother's hands and feet. "What did they do to you?"

"You know, the usual, drained my blood, poisoned me, then kicked my ass. Enough to keep me too weak to shift." Roden reported. "You're insane. You know this is a trap!"

"Think I give a fuck about a trap?" Raden finished with the ropes. "I would not leave you here to die, brother."

"How did you get in here?" Roden asked. "I don't hear anyone with you."

"I brought new friends." Raden looked up to where Kiora stood. "Ones who have more discreet methods of invasion."

"Incoming!" Kiora called out. "I feel them. They're headed this way. And it's a lot of them!"

"Alright, let's get ready for a show!" Marley boasted.

"Sounds like they need you now." Roden said. "I wish I could help, but I'm too weak."

"Don't you dare come up there? I'm coming back for you." Raden promised, then jumped out of the pit, leaving his brother alone.

Before Raden's feet touched the ground, the thunderous sound of soil moving filled the room. Kiora called the earth to block the entrance to the room and seal them inside. The mountain of stone and dirt compressed into the opening was the last barrier between their team and the approaching threat.

"That's only going to buy us another minute or two." She looked at Raden. "Now what?"

"We fight," he pointed to the others. "While you get my brother out of here."

"How?" Kiora looked around the room. "There are vampires on every side of this place. They're ready for us."

"This entire place is dirt, Kiora. Make your own exit." Roe rolled her wrist, gathering the force of air around her.

"Right, okay, but what about the rest of you?" She looked at her friends. "I can't just leave you here."

"We'll be right behind you." Roe looked at Kiora, and Kiora knew exactly what she meant.

"Elevator?" Kiora spoke of the method they developed during their training. It was their go to move whenever they were in a tough spot.

"Exactly." Roe looked at the doorway where the rock crumbled, and the sound of fists pummeled against the compacted earth.

"Brilliant!" Kiora beamed.

"That's why you brought me with you." Roe winked at her.

A second later, the reinforced barrier that the vampires out fell, creating a space large enough for one person to get through at a time while the others continued beating at the wall to break it down further.

Roe and Sky immediately used their control of the air to knock back any vampire who pushed through the small opening. It worked until they knocked more of the wall down and allowed more vampires to enter. That's when Marley jumped into action, shooting flames that set the attackers on fire. Their agonizing screams echoed in the room.

Soon the opening was large enough for multiple vampires, all flashing fangs, to get through. They charged the fairies that tried to keep them at bay.

"Kiora, my brother." Raden reminded her of their plan before he took off to join the fight.

"Right." Kiora hesitated before she turned to Roden. But tripped up when Raden called out. She turned to see him pinned to the ground as a vampire tried to bite into his neck. Its drool dripped onto Raden as it snapped and snarled.

"Raden!" Kiora stepped toward him.

"No," he pushed the vampire off him and quickly drove a stake through its heart. "Get him out of here. Now!"

She looked around the room and, though she wanted to help him; she realized she couldn't risk the mission. This was what she trained for. To protect those who couldn't protect themselves. Roden was the priority, and she had to get him out.

Just as she reached the edge of the pit, she turned and saw something that pissed her off. Marius cowered away from the fight. He didn't help the others at all, but oddly enough; the vampires weren't attacking him. If she had the time to confront him, she would have. Instead, she leapt off the edge of the pit.

"Roden?" Kiora approached the wolf carefully. "My name is Kiora. I'm a friend of your brother's. I'm here to help you get out of here."

"Kiora?" Roden repeated her name.

"Yes," she bent to look him in the face. "I'm here."

"Thank you." he said, a tear falling from his eye.

"Thank me after I get you out of here." She winked at him.

Raden was far too heavy for her to lift him out of the pit. Instead, she knelt beside him, touching the earth to request its power. The ground beneath them rumbled as a small platform formed under the chair where Roden sat.

"We're getting out of here." She whispered, and the platform rose, the earth stretching to lift them toward the domed ceiling.

As they rose, Kiora held on to Roden to keep him stable. Until the shriek of a vampire called her attention. She turned just in time to defend herself against the blood sucker. Kiora's left foot contacted the vampire's jaw, which sent it flying backward. A moment later, another vampire attacked, but instead of kicking it, she used the earth and sent bullet sized rocks through its chest and skull.

The platform reached a point just high enough for her to touch the ceiling with her hand.

"Open." Kiora said, and the ceiling opened, creating a shaft that reached up to the surface. The support beneath the platform crumbled as the sides met the new shaft, and the makeshift elevator took her and Roden out of the underground cavern and away from the sounds of the continuing fight.

Ten

They weren't safe above ground. With the sun setting, the vampires and their familiars were already prepared to attack. Instead of risking the battle head on, Kiora created a dome of compacted dirt around her and Roden with just enough opening so she could see when the others came out of the hole, she left behind her.

A minute after she exited, Marley's vibrant wings carried him up the shaft and with him came a wave of flames that burned everyone in its path.

"That was amazing." Kiora dropped the dome.

"Well, you know I like to put on a good show." Marley took a bow. "Let's get him out of here."

"The others?" Kiora watched as Marley helped Roden to his feet and draped the wolf's arm over his shoulder.

"They'll be fine. We have our directive. Get the injured wolf out of here." he pointed to the wall of flames that kept the vampires back. "That will not last forever."

"You're right. Okay." Kiora took Roden's other arm and draped it over her shoulder. "Let's get out of here."

They flew two miles to the north before Kiora opened the ground again. Once beneath the surface, they traveled the same as they had before, back to the hideout, where they would wait for the others to arrive. It was no surprise to either of them that Marius, the coward who hadn't aided in their fight, was the first to show up.

Next was Sky, and then shortly after her, Roe.

"We can't wait forever." Marius said.

"No," Kiora said firmly. "We're waiting for him."

"What if he doesn't come?" Roe asked. "I'm on your side here, Kiora, but the vampires will look for us. It's not safe for us to be here for too long."

"I know. I'm monitoring their movement. They're nowhere near us. He will come." She looked at Roden, who lay on the ground next to her. "You can feel him, right? He's okay, right?"

"I'm weak." Roden shook his head. "I could barely feel him before and it's still faint."

"So that means he might be dead." Marius said. "We need to get the hell out of here."

"No, I refuse to believe that." Kiora stood from her position next to Roden. "Roe, please keep an eye on him. I'm going back for Raden."

"Are you insane?" Marius spoke up. "We barely made it out of there the first time."

"Actually, it looked like you didn't really have an issue getting out." Marley rolled a flame across his fingertips. "I mean, look at you. The rest of us are all beat up and you stand there without a scratch."

"Yeah, come to think of it, I didn't see you fighting at all." Roe turned on Marius. "What the hell is up with that?"

"What are you trying to imply?" Marius' eyes shifted between the others.

"That you're a traitor, obviously." Sky laughed. "I mean, it doesn't take a genius to figure that out."

"I-"

"Whatever, I'm going back." Kiora moved. "Don't let him anywhere near Roden."

"No, you aren't!" Marius grabbed Kiora's arm, yanking her so hard that she slammed into the wall.

"What the hell?" Marley pushed Marius and Marius returned a blow of air to Marley's chest, knocking him out.

"Are you out of you mind?" Sky ran to Marley's side.

"I'm taking Kiora home. We're done here!" Marius reached for Kiora again, but before his hand touched her a deafening growl came from the open tunnel just a moment before the wolf burst into the small spaced. Paws planted in the fairy's chest as Raden's bared teeth threatened to take off his head.

Fur became skin as Raden transformed from wolf to man again. One hand gripped Marius' collar while the other, balled into a fist, slammed into his jaw.

"Didn't I tell you I'd rip your fucking head off?" Raden threatened.

"Raden!" Kiora called his name. "You're alive."

"I am." He looked over his shoulder at her for a moment before returning his attention to the man he held down. He punched Marius again, hard enough to draw blood. "Where's my brother?"

"Here." Roden said weakly. "I'm right here."

"Are you okay?" Raden asked.

"I will be." Roden responded. "In time."

"We need to get you home." Raden said and moved his hand to wrap around Marius' neck to keep him pinned.

"You want to let me go while you have this little chat?" Marius choked.

"No." Raden snapped at him.

"How are you going to get him home?" Roe asked. "I doubt we can stay out here until the sun rises again."

"We're going to have to. Seal this place back up and be prepared for whatever comes, but help is coming. I put the call out." Raden answered.

"You did?" Kiora asked. "What about the risk?"

"There is no more risk. I couldn't do it, not until I got him out of there." Raden asked. "They would have killed him if wolves descended on this place."

"I understand." Kiora nodded.

"Can you do that earth healing thing for him?" Raden pointed to his brother. "Will it work?"

"Um, yes. I can." Kiora nodded.

"Great, while you do that, I'll redress. And you," He looked at Marius. "You're going to sit in that corner and stay there. And if I even think you're trying to do some sneaky shit, I'll kill you."

"Fuck it, I'll kill him now." Marley grunted, rubbing the back of his head. "Knock me down like that again and see what happens."

"Great, two threats on your life." Sky pointed at Marius. "Think you can keep your mouth under control?"

"I'm good." Marius muttered, then moved to the corner where he sat through the night.

Kiora first opened the earth to put Roden into the healing wrap. Then she sealed off the tunnel and opened only a few air ways. With Roe and Sky there, they could pull in more than enough air for the group to survive on. Kiora kept her hand on the ground and felt for the movement of the vampires. They never came their way.

As they settled in, Raden sat next to Kiora, near his brother. He kept a watchful eye on Marius while Kiora looked at him, relieve he was okay. She couldn't help looking at Marley and Sky, who cuddled together in their own corner and inspired a longing for Kiora. She missed having someone to lean on. When she looked back at Raden, there was a pang of sorrow because she knew the next day they'd part ways.

116

He shifted, eyes still on the enemy, but his hand fell next to hers. It was close enough that she could feel the heat coming off his skin, but not enough to actually touch her. She sat in the awkward space, head and heart conflicted, and wished she could escape.

A moment later, her mind tingled, and her friend pulled her from her reality.

"Again, with this?" Kiora feigned annoyance.

"Oh, get off it, I recognized that look on your face." Roe laughed. "You wanted out of there, and I know damn well you didn't think I was going to wait until we got home to tease you about it."

"What do you have to tease me about?"

"Marius is right." She squinted at her friend. "I see it all over you now. There's something more between you and the wolf."

"Roe," Kiora shook her head. "Please don't do this."

"Hey, you saved the brother. Now it's time to be honest." Roe shrugged, and a chair appeared behind her where she sat. "I'm not saying that you came out here because of it, but you've definitely developed feelings for the man. You two are practically cuddling right now."

"We're not even touching!"

"But you want to be!" Roe pointed at her. "Admit it."

"It doesn't matter." Kiora plopped down in her own seat. "He's a wolf. I'm a fairy. And tomorrow we will go our separate ways."

"I'm hearing excuses. Weak ones at that."

"It would never work."

"So, you admit you want it to." The wide grin stretched across her face like she'd caught her friend with her hand in the cookie jar.

"Maybe." Kiora chewed her lips. "I guess. I don't know. But that is not why I'm here."

"Girl, I know you didn't let the brain between your legs talk you into risking your life. But you can't deny what's developed between you."

"He's going home, and I'm going back to Rege." Kiora repeated.

"So, you said." Roe tapped her knee. "I'll drop it for now."

"I know you want to live vicariously through me, but this isn't the story where the fairy ends up with the wolf."

"How tragic." Roe melted into the chair that reclined beneath her.

"I know." Kiora pouted.

BREAK

"Its weird right?" Roe asked as the outer wall opened up the next morning. "That the vampires didn't try to find us?"

"Hell yeah." Marley stretched. "Didn't expect them to give up so easily."

"Something more to it?" Roe questioned. "Maybe they're just buying time and they'll attack us back at home."

"In that case, we better get there before they do." Sky chimed in.

"Maybe not." Roden said as he dusted the dirt from his chest. "They're hoping the virus will have mutated enough that I will no longer understand it or be able to create a cure."

"Is that possible?" Kiora asked.

"Yes, it is. But I won't know for sure until I make it to the lab." He answered and climbed from the hole in the ground. "That is amazing, using the energy of the earth to heal. Fascinating. I would love to pick your brain about how the magic works."

"Let's just focus on getting you home." Raden patted his brother on the shoulder then looked at Kiora. "Join me outside?"

"Um, sure." Kiora glance at Roe, who gave her a suspicious look.

Outside, beneath the sun, Raden stretched his limbs. Kiora watched him until he finished.

"Did you want me to just watch your stretching routine? I supposed I could incorporate some of your movements into my own practice."

"No." he laughed. "I just wanted to thank you. Away from the others."

"You couldn't thank me near the others?"

"With all the bickering, and my desire to take the coward's head off, I figured this would be the better option." He shook his head. "The only reason that man is alive is because I want to keep the peace between our people."

"I appreciate that. We will deal with him at home."

"Good." He pointed to the cavern. "Because it took everything not to break his neck last night."

"You're welcome, by the way. Though you don't really owe me a thank you."

"Yes, I do. You put your neck out on the line for me. I owe you a lot more than that." he paused. "Is it true? What Marius said?"

"What did he say?" She bent down to sniff a wildflower.

"About your lust for me?"

"I-" she popped back up like a startled meerkat. "I don't know what you mean."

"You like me." He winked. "Or at least your jealous ex feels like you do. I'm assuming he's the crazy ex-boyfriend in the scenario."

"Yea, Marius is my ex." she nodded. "It's been over a year, but he refuses to let go. But just because he thinks the only reason I would do something kind is if I had some sort of attraction to the person, doesn't mean it's true."

"Never mind." he chuckled. "You shouldn't like me, anyway."

"Why? Because you're a wolf?" She pointed out the obvious issue.

"That," he paused. "And because I'm dying."

"What?" She stepped closer to him. "What do you mean, you're dying?"

"That virus my brother is trying to cure. I have it." Raden admitted.

"But your brother is safe now. He can develop the medicine and cure you." She rationalized.

"Maybe." Raden shrugged and looked up at the sky, stretching his arms to the warmth of the sun. "Maybe not."

"I can't believe this. Why didn't you say something sooner?"

"Because it would have clouded your judgement and made you worry about me more than you needed to." He grabbed her hand.

"Kiora, I need to say thank you. For what you've done for me."

"Of course. It's what I wanted someone to do for me." She repeated the same reasoning she'd given before.

"If it's okay with you, I'm going to tell myself it's because you liked me." Raden finished his stretches. "That there was something special about me."

"Well, since you're dying, let's just say that's the truth." She smiled, but there was an undeniable sorrow in her eyes.

"In that case," he wrapped his arm around her waist, pulling her closer to him. "I think that means I get a kiss."

"Oh?" Kiora bit her bottom lip.

Raden leaned into her, stopping just short of her lips. A pause meant to give her an option to back out, but Kiora pressed her lips against his. The ground trembled beneath their feet as the two kissed. And when they parted, Kiora had to catch her breath.

"Well, damn." she smiled. "Who knew a wolf could kiss so good?"

"I will make sure the cure gets to you." He brushed her chin. "For your friend. Our men are almost here."

"What about you?" Kiora asked. "You can bring it to me, can't you? Why are you talking like you're not going to be around?"

"I don't know that I will be." He touched her jaw. "But thanks to you, I know my brother will survive."

"I'm choosing not to think so negatively about this." She blinked to keep the tears from falling, then changed the topic. "I can feel the trucks driving in. I'll let the others know we'll be leaving soon."

Raden pulled her in for a second kiss before he let her go.

"Just in case." He winked when their lips parted.

While Kiora returned to the hideout to inform the others, Raden remained above ground. By the time the rest of the group made it back out with Roden, ten large trucks sat in front of them.

"Time for us to go, brother." Raden said as Roden walked over to him. "You've got work to do. No time to lounge around."

"Of course," Roden huffed, then turned to the others. "Thank you all for what you've done. I will not forget it."

"Just make sure you figure out that cure." Sky said.

"You owe us no thanks," Kiora shook Roden's hand before he headed for the truck with the open door.

"I'll see you around." Raden winked at Kiora.

"Yeah, I'll see you." Kiora smiled, though her voice shook with her sadness.

"Are you okay?" Roe stepped to her side when Raden walked away. "What did he say?"

"He's dying." Kiora's voice shook more, and a tear fell from her right eye. "He's sick and now there may not be enough time to save him."

"Are you serious?" Roe put her arm around Kiora. "Girl, I'm sorry."

"It's what I felt before." They watched the trucks pull away. "The earth. It took so long to heal him and even when he was okay, he wasn't a hundred percent. He's dying, Roe."

"Damn." Roe hugged her friend.

"What am I supposed to do?" Kiora looked at her.

"Enjoy it for what it is. You helped him. That's what matters." She reassured her. "You did what you set out to do. And a lot of people may benefit from it. You may have just helped save a ton of lives, Kiora."

"Yeah, you're right. Let's go home."

Eleven

Three weeks later, a package arrived in Rege with Kiora's name on it. Inside was a vial of medicine and a note.

My brother asked that you get this. More will arrive soon.

Thank you.

~Roden

Kiora read the note several times, hoping the message would change. The name signed to the card would have an 'a' and not an 'o'. But of course, it didn't. She kept hoping she would hear from him but returned to her routine of guarding the boundaries of Rege. After their involvement with rescuing Roden, the fairies were concerned that the vampires would attack.

The medicine worked as hoped. Soon after taking it, Max was back to herself and restored in her position as a superior. Unfortunately, nothing happened to Marius despite their suspicions of him. Even after Kiora filed reports against him. They just sent him out on another convoy. At least he was away from her.

Months later, not one vampire had stepped foot on their territory, but Max and the other superiors were still on high alert. Reports of activity outside of Rege caused suspicions that the vampires were making a play, but no one knew what it was.

"Are you still waiting for him to show up?" Roe approached Kiora outside the towers.

"No, I don't think so." Kiora said unconvincingly.

"What's going on?" Roe laced her fingers with Kiora's. "Talk to me."

"I kept telling myself that he was just taking time to heal. You saw how long it took Max to get back on her feet even after she took the cure." Kiora revealed her inner thoughts.

"You don't think that anymore?"

"It's been months, Roe." She dropped her head back. "We know the wolves have a period of mourning. I suspect soon they will announce his death."

"I'm sorry, Kiora." Roe squeezed her hand. "I wish there was more I could do."

"It was wishful thinking, anyway. Not like we were going to be together. He was a wolf. I'm a fairy. Even with the recent steps towards peace, no one would accept the son of the alpha being with me."

"He didn't strike me as the type of man to care what anyone else had to say about who he spent his time with." Roe said. "I

125

mean you see how he attacked Marius anytime he came at you the wrong way. He'd fight for you."

"Which further confirms that he isn't around anymore to fight for me." Kiora frowned. "It's okay, I'll be fine. We should really get inside. Max is back, and I doubt she'll excuse any tardiness."

"This has to be a big deal, right?" Roe said as they walked into the room. "I mean, all the superiors have been called back and they've more than tripled the number of guards in the last six months. Something's going down, and soon."

"Let's not speculate, please." Kiora waved off Roe's conspiracy theory.

"Right, we should just wait until they tell us how our lives are going to change again." Roe nudged her in the side before the two headed inside.

Inside the room was buzzing with whispered rumors. Kiora looked around and noticed a few key people were missing, namely Doni, her bully. Instead of listening to the hushed conversations, she took her seat next to Roe and focused on the head of the room. A moment later, Max, followed by five other superiors, entered and took the bench.

"Listen up, people." Max called out. "This will not be a normal meeting. We have your reports, and as soon as we're done, you'll go about your business as usual."

"Woah, what's up with that?" Roe whispered.

Kiora shook her head and shrugged. "No clue."

"You may notice some of your colleagues are missing today and there are fresh faces among our ranks. That is why we are here. I'm not proud to report to you we've found that some of our partners, our brothers and sisters of the guard, were working in alliance with the vampires."

The room filled with the noise of disbelief and questions.

"How can you be sure?" someone called out.

"We have a guest here today who will give more information about that." Max answered and pointed to the back of the crescent-shaped room.

On cue, the doors at the back of the room opened and everyone hushed as werewolves, all dressed in black suits, marched into the room.

Roe grabbed Kiora's arm and Kiora turned to the door but said nothing.

Twenty wolves entered, lining either side of the room and then nothing else. She scanned every face but recognized none of them.

Kiora turned to face Max again but snapped her head back when someone kicked Marius into the room. He rolled down the steps and landed on the floor in front of Max. Blood dripped from his back and Kiora covered the gasp as she realized his wings had been cut. It was the ultimate punishment for a fairy to have their wings removed.

"What the hell?" Roe asked.

"I don't know." Kiora looked at Roe and then the sound of footsteps drew her attention back to the door where a new person appeared wearing a white suit with gold accents. Raden.

"Girl!" Roe gripped Kiora's arm tighter and shook it. "That's your man!"

"Shush!" Kiora looked at her with bugged out eyes.

Raden took careful steps as he approached the bench. He passed her but didn't look at her. He kept his eyes on Max and the traitor on the floor in front of her.

"Raden. Thank you for joining us." Max greeted him.

"Of course," he said.

"Please tell us your findings."

"This man, you know him as Marius, but we've known him for a few years as the Marksman. He's been working with the vampires and has recruited quite a few of your people into his rebellion. It was his hope, like many others, to weaponize the virus and use it to take power for himself. He planned to start by replacing your superiors, one by one, and then work his way up the food chain to the high court."

"He wanted to kill the Queen?" Roe asked.

"We believe so, yes." Raden found her voice and then the woman next to her.

"That's probably where Doni is." Roe muttered.

"Damn." Kiora whispered. "Now we know why he was always in my face. Reporting back to Marius."

"It took us years to crack this case, which has ultimately led us to the revelation of many other entities working with the vampires. Please don't take this as a negative mark on your people. There are rotten apples in every area, and we are determined to track them all down." Raden continued. "I'd like to take this time to give recognition to one of your brave guards, without whom this wouldn't have happened. Kiora."

The room clapped and Kiora felt her chest swell with pride. The others doubted her abilities since she joined. They thought Max showed her favor, and because of that, few took her seriously. Maybe that acknowledgement would change things. Her eyes met Raden, and he winked at her.

"Alright everyone, you heard the man. There are snakes in the grass. Keep your eyes open and protect our home." Max called out. "Back to work, people."

Kiora couldn't move. As the others filed out of the meeting room, she watched Raden hand Marius over to Max, then turn and leave ahead of the other wolves. He hadn't looked at her again. Roe said something to her, but she couldn't hear the witty comment over her own internal thoughts.

She considered that Raden no longer felt about her like she did about him. That he hadn't spent the last few months thinking of her and wishing they were together. She waited for him to return to her. Thought he would come back into the meeting room to talk to her about what he'd been up to. He didn't. She had to consider that maybe for him she was just as wishful thought of a dying wolf. Raden was not the same man she knew.

"Kiora," Max was the one to return.

"Glad to see you back on your feet." Kiora stood as Max approached her. "Melanin is glowing once again."

"Thanks to you, though that recovery process was a pain in the ass." Max laughed. "Why are you still here? You should go home to rest."

"I should, yes." Kiora chewed her lip.

"And yet you're here."

"I thought he was dead, Max." She led with honesty.

"I know." Max placed her hand on Kiora's arm.

"You knew he wasn't." Kiora knew when Max was hiding something from her.

"Yes." Max admitted. "I did."

"Why didn't you tell me?"

"Because as much as I love you, I couldn't risk losing the opportunity. To catch a traitor. As far as Marius knew, Raden died after he left. Watching you mourn the wolf only confirmed that. If you knew he was okay, it would have been obvious."

"Glad my pain proved beneficial for you all." She sucked her teeth.

"I apologize for your pain, but not for what I did. This was a major break for us." Max said honestly. "You're a part of the guard. Your pain was an unfortunate byproduct of the job."

"Right." Kiora sat back down.

"Kiora, he's not coming back here. There is a lot more that needs to be done out there. I know that's why you're here."

"I know you're right, but the moment I walk out of here, I have to let whatever thoughts I had of him go. You know?" She laced her fingers together. "It will really be over then. Because it won't be death keeping him away. It will be a choice he made."

"And you're not ready to do that?"

"No, believe it or not, I'm not ready." Kiora wiped the tear from her eye.

"Take your time." Max touched her knee. "And thank you again for everything you did to help us get to this point."

"Of course, it's my job."

Max left the room and Kiora sat alone for another hour before she left the meeting room. She told herself when the door shut behind her; it was the end. She'd let Raden go for good.

She took the long way home, flying across Rege and looking down at the city she called home. It no longer felt like home, just a place where she had a duty. A job. To protect the citizens. The love she had for the land, the connection she felt to the people, it faded each day. Before she turned back toward her home, she made a promise to herself to open her heart and her mind again. She would find that love, that connection again. Even if it meant leaving Rege to do so.

She landed in front of the main house. Where her parents lived. During the months since she held Raden, she'd moved into the larger home. Thought it would make her feel better or reconnected to her home. It didn't. If anything, it pushed her closer to her decision to leave. Knowing that it would be one of her last nights in Rege, she headed towards the smaller building in the back. The home her father built for her.

Two steps from the door, a deep voice called her name and Kiora screamed, flew back twenty feet, and shot ten earth bullets into the darkness.

"Kiora! Stop!" The voice called again and that time she recognized it.

"Raden?" she huffed. "What the hell?"

"I thought I would surprise you." He stepped out of the shadows. "Clearly a mistake."

"I thought you were dead." Kiora caught her breath. "Now you're sneaking up on me. Don't do that."

"I know, I'm sorry, but we figured that was the best way." He rubbed his jaw where one of her projectiles hit him in the face. "Dammit, that hurt."

"Sorry, but you scared the hell out of me." She paused. "Max told me everything. Thank you for sending the cure for her."

"I told you I would." He winked. "I keep my word. It matters."

"So, Marius." Kiora leaned into the awkward conversation. "When did you figure out he was a traitor?"

"The moment I smelled him. It made sense that they had helped. A lot of the things they've been doing lately were outside of their natural abilities." Raden explained. "I'd suspected it for a while. Didn't think he'd be dumb enough to walk right up to me."

"You think there are others?"

"I know there are, and not just fairies. This is a bigger problem."

"What now?" Kora asked. "Are you going after them?"

"Yes, I plan to track down as many of the traitors as I can." Raden said. "Marius was an easy one to crack. Didn't take long before he started spilling all kinds of secrets."

"Oh," she said, disappointed because it meant they still wouldn't be together. At least he was alive.

"And you're coming with me." Raden walked across the yard to her.

"What?" She looked up at him. "I am?"

"I put in a special request as a part of the new alliance between our people that I be allowed to work with a team of my choosing. Both wolf and fairy." The hint of a smile touched his lips. He wanted her by his side.

"And you chose me? A rookie?" She smirked. "Don't you want someone with more experience?"

"I want you." He moved closer, leaving an inch of space between them. "Best damn rookie, I know."

"Wow." She fought to keep her cool, even though she wanted to jump into his arms. "I guess I should be flattered."

"Unless you don't want to come with me. You're free to remain in Rege with your people." He clarified. "I won't force you to come. This is going to be dangerous, even more than what we've already faced."

"Will you be there?" she asked.

"Well, yeah." He chuckled. "I wouldn't send you off with anyone else. Like I said, I want you by *my* side."

"Honestly, there's not much here for me but echoes of a life I don't even want to live anymore."

"So, you'll come with me?" Raden stepped closer to her, wrapped his arm around her waist.

"Is this a professional trip or a personal one?"

"We can blend the two." he growled, kissed her, then lifted her into his arms.

Kiora's mind raced and her heart soared as the wolf carried the fairy into the home she'd leave behind in the favor of danger.

Author Bio

Jessica Cage is an International Award Winning, and USA Today Bestselling Author from Chicago, IL. As a girl, Jessica enjoyed reading tales of fantasy and mystery, but she always hoped to find characters that looked like her. Those characters came few and far in between. When they appeared they often played a minor role and were background figures. This is the inspiration for her independent publishing journey and the reason she focuses on writing **Characters of Color in Fantasy.** Representation matters in all mediums and Jessica is determined to give the young girl who looks like her, a story full of characters that she can relate to. Jessica has independently published over thirty titles and has been featured in fifteen different anthologies to date. Jessica recently signed with WEBTOON to produce exclusive content for their new reading app, YONDER.